"You'd better looked serious.

She turned on him. "Strip? What do you mean, strip?"

"I mean remove your clothes."

"Whatever for?"

"To get the skunk smell off your skin," he explained patiently. "You've got to soak in tomato juice, and there's no point wasting it on that uniform. It'll have to be burned."

He could see how reluctantly her hands rose to take off her jacket. Then her skirt. He didn't want to think about how weird it was to ogle a woman who smelled as she did right now.

The skunk episode was one thing. But even worse, he lusted after her. And that was the biggest catastrophe of all.

Dear Reader,

We have two very different but equally enjoyable LOVE & LAUGHTER stories this month.

Bestselling Harlequin Romance author Patricia Knoll pens #53 *Delightful Jones,* a charming tale of a butler on an Arizona ranch. The last thing cowboy Tyler Morris thinks his home needs is a butler. The fact that the butler is female only makes matters worse. His ranch is for cattle and horses, not champagne and caviar. But Erin Jones is determined to do the job for which she was hired. A battle of sexes and life-styles ensues!

Then for a complete change of pace, enjoy a real screwball romance, #54 *Right Chapel, Wrong Couple* by Colleen Collins. Set in Las Vegas, it features a runaway bride, an impromptu wedding, gangsters, jewels, showgirls and just about everything else! America On Line, Romance Reader had this to say about Colleen's first book. "Some of the Love & Laughter books are destined to be classics. Colleen Collins's new book (*Right Chest, Wrong Name*) is going to be remembered for having some of the most humorous, genuinely witty lines around. Her use of dialogue, sharp and crisp, is going to be remembered, too. Frankly, I am in awe. This author is a rising star."

Have a good time and enjoy both books!

Malle Vallik

Malle Vallik
Associate Senior Editor

DELIGHTFUL JONES
Patricia Knoll

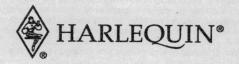

HARLEQUIN®

TORONTO • NEW YORK • LONDON
AMSTERDAM • PARIS • SYDNEY • HAMBURG
STOCKHOLM • ATHENS • TOKYO • MILAN • MADRID
PRAGUE • WARSAW • BUDAPEST • AUCKLAND

If you purchased this book without a cover you should be aware that this book is stolen property. It was reported as "unsold and destroyed" to the publisher, and neither the author nor the publisher has received any payment for this "stripped book."

ISBN 0-373-44053-7

DELIGHTFUL JONES

Copyright © 1998 by Patricia Knoll

All rights reserved. Except for use in any review, the reproduction or utilization of this work in whole or in part in any form by any electronic, mechanical or other means, now known or hereafter invented, including xerography, photocopying and recording, or in any information storage or retrieval system, is forbidden without the written permission of the publisher, Harlequin Enterprises Limited, 225 Duncan Mill Road, Don Mills, Ontario, Canada M3B 3K9.

All characters in this book have no existence outside the imagination of the author and have no relation whatsoever to anyone bearing the same name or names. They are not even distantly inspired by any individual known or unknown to the author, and all incidents are pure invention.

This edition published by arrangement with Harlequin Books S.A.

® and TM are trademarks of the publisher. Trademarks indicated with ® are registered in the United States Patent and Trademark Office, the Canadian Trade Marks Office and in other countries.

Printed in U.S.A.

A funny thing happened...

Victor Hugo said on his deathbed that dying was easy, writing comedy was hard. I don't know about that, but I have discovered that writing comedy is hard but fun. There are moments when characters and incidents come together to create good comic scenes that I hope will bring the readers a laugh.

When I first read a magazine article about a school for butlers, I thought it would be funny to have a girl butler working on a ranch—like Bob Hope's character in the old movie *Fancy Pants*. As I thought about the scrapes she could get into with a hardworking rancher, the idea grew and the characters of Erin Jones and Tyler Morris were born.

I called upon my many years as a teacher and a mother of four to create situations for Junior and Bucky, the little neighbor boys in *Delightful Jones,* though, of course *my* children would never have done some of the things these boys do!

I hope you enjoy this trip to Arizona and the characters I've created there.

Happy reading!

Patricia Knoll

Don't miss Patricia Knoll's next book in the MARRIAGE TIES miniseries from Harlequin Romance. Wedding Bells will be available in November 1998 wherever books are sold.

1

SHE HEARD THE SCREAMING first.

Erin Jones had just stepped from her car when she heard what sounded like the shrieking of small children nearby. She had been checking her appearance, smoothing her gray-striped skirt, donning her black suit jacket and making sure every one of her wild blond hairs was tucked into the bun on top of her head.

She glanced quickly around the curving graveled driveway that led to the redbrick ranch house, across the highway to a tumbledown shack, then beyond to a field planted in alfalfa.

She couldn't see anyone, but she could still hear the screaming—and it was coming closer.

Erin leaned into the car to get her keys and purse from the seat. Before she could grab them, she glanced up and saw two little boys stumble around the corner of the house.

She watched in astonishment as they struggled toward her. They were yelling and pushing against each other, then doubling their fists, they pummeled each other's heads. After each had gotten in a few good licks, they lurched around to bawl at something behind them. They yawed from side to side as if they were drunken men in a three-legged race. Even though their short limbs churned the ground and they seemed to be trying to run, they were held back.

After a stunned instant, Erin realized that they were tied together by a rope and that something was holding the other end. The harder they tried to run, the tighter the rope got, and the more entangled they became. Finally they tripped over each other's feet and down they went, rolling in the dirt, still shrieking and throwing punches.

Leaving the car door standing open, Erin ran to help.

"Hey," she said, reaching for them. "What's going on?"

She bent to grab the rope, hoping to free them. When they caught sight of her, they began to yell even louder. They tried to squirm away, but were handicapped by the rope, which was now looped twice around them. It ran between one boy's legs, then up to hook around the other one's shoulders.

"Stop wiggling," she commanded sharply, trying to wedge her fingers beneath the knot. They didn't listen, but she had been raised with three brothers and knew how to hold her own with boys. She grasped the rope close to the two squirming bodies and jerked it toward them, hoping to gain some slack so she could untangle them. When she snapped the rope, which was still stretched taut around the corner of the house, she heard a loud clatter. The rope suddenly went loose.

Relieved that she had unhooked it from whatever had been holding it, Erin wound the rope under and around the pint-size prisoners, then discovered that it was pulled into a hard knot.

She began working to loosen it. As soon as the

rope had gone limp, the boys had stopped shrieking, but they continued to wiggle and push at each other, making her job harder.

"How did you get tied up like this?" she asked the taller of the two who didn't look to be much older than seven. The other boy was younger by a year or two. They had blond hair sticking up in spikes, blue eyes puffy from crying and were dressed alike in jeans and white T-shirts. Their faces were smeared with identical quantities of dirt, tears and bits of hay.

"He roped us," the older one said, taking a swipe at his runny nose.

"Who did?" Erin asked.

The boy's bottom lip stuck out and fresh tears welled into his eyes. "We were just goin' into the barn to play with the kittens and he came out of the house yellin' and swingin' that rope. He roped us like we was cows and he hurt us." The tears began to flow down the youngster's cheeks.

Erin was appalled, unable to imagine who would have done such a thing. She patted his shoulder. "Now, don't cry. Whoever roped you like this will be punished."

His lips trembled as the little boy looked up. "You promise?"

"Yes. Now, who was it?" she asked, looking down at the older boy as she finally removed the last coil of rope.

The boy jerked his chin. "Him."

Erin frowned and pointed to the smaller boy. "Not this little guy."

The bigger boy looked past her and screamed, "No, *him!*" The two of them shot away from her, leaped into her car, slammed the door, then scrambled around locking all four doors.

Her mouth agape, Erin stared at them, then swung around to see a man coming around the corner of the house. He was tall and dark-haired, with a murderous expression in his black eyes, a cast on his right leg and a pair of crutches under his arms. He was carrying the other end of the rope, which was looped into big coils. He threw it down in disgust when he saw that the boys were free.

"Who the hell are you?" he demanded as he stumped forward. His gaze raked over her once, dismissively. "Did you untie those little pyromaniacs?"

Erin straightened, reacting automatically to his tone. "Well, yes, I..."

"Why didn't you mind your own business? Where are...oh, there they are. Good. They're trapped." He moved past her with surprising speed and stopped at the car. "Is this yours?"

"Yes." Finally gathering her wits, Erin scooted up beside him.

"Unlock it," the man ordered. "I need to talk to these two."

"Wait a minute." Erin held up both hands. "Wait just a minute. These boys were tied up with a rope. They said they had been hurt."

"I'm glad to hear it," he answered with relish, fury snapping in his eyes.

"Did you rope them?"

"I'm happy to say I did," he answered, sticking his chin out belligerently. "They were trying to burn down my barn!"

Erin gave him a skeptical look. "Oh, now really. I don't think two little boys would..."

"Oh, yes they would. They try it every time they think I'm not looking—not that it's any of your business, lady." He reached out with one hand and rattled the door handle. "Now unlock this damned door!"

"Well, really," she protested, but his angry tone had her slapping her hand against her pocket, then starting in dismay. She spun around to see that the older boy had found the keys and was fitting them into the ignition.

"If Earl Junior can reach the gas pedal, lady, you're going to have to kiss your car goodbye," the man growled. "He'll drive it into the desert and have it stripped down in about ten seconds flat."

Erin sprang for the door and began rapping on the window. "Unlock this door immediately!"

Both boys ignored her. The younger one was busy upending her purse onto the seat and pawing through the contents. He scooped a handful of coins out of her change purse and into his pocket, then with a crow of delight, he latched onto a piece of chewing gum. He was reaching for Erin's wallet when the bigger boy, Earl, glanced around and made a dive for the stick of gum. A battle ensued that roiled from the bucket seats in front, to the one behind, then back again.

At last, Earl Junior grabbed the gum, whipped off the wrapper and stuffed it into his mouth. Seemingly having forgotten about starting the car, he sat on the steering wheel and bounced, blowing the horn each time his bottom landed.

Shrieking in anger and frustration, the younger boy threw himself against Earl, whacked him a few good licks, then scrambled for the door handle. Seeing her opportunity, Erin skipped around the car and grabbed the door just as the little boy opened it. He shoved past her and ran off down the driveway.

"Bucky, come back here!" the man bellowed, but the child kept running.

Before Erin could begin to get the other boy out, she saw a movement out of the corner of her eye. A woman had walked onto the porch.

Because she was already off-balance by the number of shocks she had experienced in the past five minutes, Erin's good manners deserted her. Her jaw dropped and her eyes widened as she looked at the newcomer.

The woman had gorgeous long legs displayed to advantage in spike heels, a short red skirt that looked as if it had been spray-painted on and a halter top that allowed plenty of room for her generous bosom to overflow. Her red hair was puffed and teased into artful curls that cascaded down her back. She held the door open and stepped forward so that one breast was thrust out at a provocative angle.

She batted heavily mascaraed eyelashes while calling out in a playful tone, "Now, Tyler, you've been on that leg too much. You need to come lie down for a while." Her sultry look implied that she was perfectly willing to lie down with him.

His face reddened and he bellowed over the honking horn. "Lie down! Shara, are you crazy? I just caught your sons trying to burn down my barn." He took a book of matches from his pocket and waved them at her. "See?"

"Now, Tyler," she soothed coyly. "They were just playing. Boys will be boys, you know."

"In this case, boys will be hellions if you don't get them under control."

Shara let the door slam behind her as she stepped forward. She plopped her hands onto her hips. "You have your nerve, Tyler. You know it's not easy for me to take care of them with Earl gone, and—"

He cut her off as if he'd heard it all before. "Junior's about to wear out this car horn. Can't you hear?"

Shara's lips drew together and she tossed her mane of hair over her shoulder. "You don't have to get mad about it. We were only trying to help you get through your troubles. I even made you some chicken soup." She flounced down the stairs, her breasts bouncing with each step and came to the car. She rapped on the window and spoke to the boy inside. "Come on, sugar. We know when we're not wanted."

"I should be so lucky," Tyler muttered. He shifted away from the car so she could get the door open, gritting his teeth as he moved.

While Erin watched, the woman pulled her son from the car ignoring the boy's screaming protests. As she dragged him down the driveway, he turned and stuck his tongue out at Tyler, yelling, "Me and Bucky didn't want you for our daddy, anyway."

"Then I've escaped a fate worse than death," Tyler answered.

Erin watched Shara sway down the driveway on her spike heels. "Do they live close by?" she asked, unable to picture the woman walking far in those shoes without crippling herself.

"Much too close," Tyler said, nodding to the shack across the road. He turned toward his own

house and began moving up the shallow steps using
one foot and both crutches, lifting his casted leg out
of the way as he progressed slowly toward the front
door. Watching him struggle, Erin tried to imagine
how he had managed to rope the two boys since he
couldn't even stand up without the aid of the
crutches.

The dust on the cast and on the seat of his jeans
told Erin that the clattering noise she had heard when
she pulled on the rope had been him falling to the
ground. She gave him an uneasy look, hoping he
didn't realize she was the one who had made him
fall. This was turning out to be enough of a fiasco
without that worsening things further.

Feeling as though she had just come through a
whirlwind, Erin pulled her suitcase from the back
seat, dumped everything back into her purse, then
grabbed it and her keys. Thinking Junior and Bucky
might pay a return visit, she locked the car, then
hurried up the steps to help Tyler.

"Here, I'll get the door for you." She set her suitcase on the porch, then hurried around him and with
a smooth motion, pushed the front door wide-open.

Tyler shuffled inside, turned and hooked the tip of
his right crutch behind the door. Erin was brought
up short by the grim expression on his face.

"Thank you," he growled. "Whatever you're selling, I don't want any, now go away."

"Selling...?" Erin shot her hand out to stop the
door that was about to be slammed in her face.
"Wait, Mr. Morris...."

The door opened again and he glared down at her.
Erin took a deep breath. Dark hair, dark eyes, dark

disposition. Yup, Tyler Morris was exactly as Miss Eugenia had described him.

His eyes swept over her, taking in the curly blond hair which she could feel slipping from the knot on top of her head, her neat suit, white blouse with its Peter Pan collar and sensible low-heeled black pumps.

Erin had expected to be welcomed and ushered inside, but the little altercation with Junior and Bucky had destroyed that possibility. At the moment, Tyler looked as though he'd rather invite scurvy into his home.

"I told you," he said in a voice devoid of even a semblance of civility. "Whatever you're selling, I don't want to buy."

Once again, he started to shut the door, but this time, Erin was ready for him. Her foot shot into the narrowing crack. "Mr. Morris, please wait."

The door closed on her foot. Erin grunted in pain, sure she could feel the bones snapping like matchsticks. "Listen to me," she gasped through gritted teeth. "Your aunt, Eugenia Morris, sent me."

There, she thought as he eased back on the door. That should do it. She knew he loved his aunt and Miss Eugenia had assured her that he would do anything for her.

Ignoring the painful throbbing in her foot, she summoned her most professional air and blessed him with a confident smile.

The door swung wide and he gazed out. His face had taken on a long-suffering look. With a sigh, he stepped onto the porch. Now that things had calmed down and she had his full attention, Erin took a moment to get a good look at him. James Westin said a person could learn a great deal about their new employer in the first few minutes if they knew what to look for.

Tyler Morris was taller than she was by at least six inches. His hair was nearly black with touches of gray at the temples, and looked as if he combed it by running his hands through it every once in a while. Impatient, Erin concluded. His eyes were of the deepest brown, shadowed by thick brows and drawn together in a frown. As she had first thought— a bad disposition. She sighed inwardly. Well, at least this job was short-term.

Erin felt her assured smile slip a notch. His looks alone would have been enough to intimidate her even without the three-day growth of beard that darkened his jaw and the long white cast that encased his right leg. He wore a pair of faded jeans that had one leg cut off high up on his thigh. The frayed ends trailed over the top of the cast.

He curled his big hands around the cross braces of the crutches, balanced himself and loomed forward. "She's found a new religion, hasn't she?" His contemptuous gaze swept over her suit, then down to the suitcase on the porch. "And you're here to move right in and convert me."

Erin stared. "Excuse me?"

"What does your group do? Worship Mount Graham?" He continued, nodding toward the highest peak of the Pinaleno Mountains to the north. "Make annual pilgrimages to sit naked on a mesa in Sedona? Kiss coyotes? Whatever it is, I'm not interested. That last bunch she got involved with nearly got away with half her life savings before I caught on to what they were doing and put a stop to it. If you've got any plans like that..."

"No. I'm not from some religious group. Mr. Morris, if you'll just listen to me for a moment, I'll explain. I'm Erin. Erin Jones."

When his fierce expression didn't change, she forged ahead. "Doris Jones is my mother. You know her, don't you?"

"Eugenia's housekeeper." Suddenly his eyes snapped wide. "Good Lord, you're that kid with the pierced eyebrow!" He leaned forward to examine her more closely and Erin resisted the urge to clap her hands over her face. Tyler's gaze swept over her, from head to toe. "Aren't you?"

Erin felt her smile flash-freeze at the same time that the heat of embarrassment flushed her face a bright red. "Well...I...the earring's gone now..." she wheezed out. "The hole has even closed up."

"Healed, you mean," he stated. "Good thing, too. It looked stupid."

That's exactly what Erin's brothers had said, which was why she'd still worn it for months after she'd grown tired of it.

"I take it that means you've...seen me before?" Dismayed, Erin tried to recall having met him at Miss Eugenia's, but couldn't. Unless he had been the one with Miss Eugenia one day when she'd been visiting her mother at work. Two people had been watching her from an upstairs window when she'd been going through a particularly rebellious stage around her eighteenth birthday.

"Hell, yes." His voice rumbled as he scrutinized her hair. "The last time I saw you, you were riding a Honda motorcycle and your hair was dyed purple."

"Magenta," she said weakly. Her heart sank. Yes, he'd been the one.

Darn! Why hadn't she thought of this? He visited Miss Eugenia's home in Tucson several times a year. Of course, there was a chance he might have seen her. She should have guessed his aunt would have told him all about her. Miss Eugenia was a gregarious lady, who had delighted in Erin's more colorful escapades—and obviously reported them to her nephew.

"Hey, did your mother ever let you get your boyfriend's name tattooed on your——?"

"No." Erin broke in hastily. Good grief. How much had her mother discussed her with Miss Eugenia? Her hands closed into fists and, with iron determination, she brought the subject back where she wanted it. "Miss Eugenia hired me to work for you."

Tyler sighed. "Oh hell, I should have known she'd send somebody. Exactly what is it you're supposed to do? Take me across country on the back of your Honda?" He adjusted his crutches and bent over to rap his knuckles against the cast. "Sorry, can't go."

This wasn't turning out at all as she had expected, but she had learned that she could handle most anything if she didn't panic.

Erin resumed her professional smile. She knew it had just the right touch of superior self-confidence because she had practiced it before the mirror to make sure it did. "I'm your new butler."

2

THIS ANNOUNCEMENT was greeted by a very long silence. Tyler's expression didn't change by so much as a millimeter. Erin wondered if he'd been through so much already today, that nothing else could surprise him.

Finally he said, "Excuse me, did you say 'butler'?"

"That's right."

"You?" His voice bobbled as if a laugh was trying to cut loose.

Erin's smile grew as brittle as parchment and her chin came up. Well, he didn't have to make it sound so ludicrous. "Yes," she answered tightly. "You mean she didn't tell you?"

His mouth drew down in a considering frown. "Nooo. Not a word."

Erin's breath puffed out. "Why, I...I can't believe it. She said she would call and tell you all about it...."

"Welcome to the ranks of the Eugenianized," he muttered.

"What do you mean?"

He tilted his head to one side as he gave her a pitying look. "I'm sure you know that she marches to a tune all her own. The rest of us don't hear it. We don't even know what's playing. She knew I wouldn't want you here so she didn't tell me you were coming."

"I...I don't understand."

"Never mind," he said darkly. "I do."

Erin floundered for a moment before pulling herself together. "Well...as I said, I'm your new butler...and if you could just tell me—"

"Miss Jones, you really don't get it, do you?" he asked. "I don't want you here. Whoever heard of a woman butler? What the hell would I want with one? And why would I want you of all people?"

That last question had a hot reply shooting to her lips, but Erin bit it back. It was a struggle, but she forced herself to recall Mr. Westin's advice about never getting into an argument with the employer. There was only one loser in such disagreements, and it wasn't the employer.

Although Erin felt as if the ground had dropped from beneath her feet, she forged on. "I've been hired to run your household, organize your schedule, take care of your social responsibilities."

"My social responsibilities." At that, Tyler threw back his head and laughed. The mocking sound rolled out over the desert. "I don't have social responsibilities. I don't even have a social *life*. What I do have is a snapped leg bone."

"Yes, I know. Miss Eugenia said you just got out of the hospital. That's why she sent me...."

"Look over there," he went on, just as if she hadn't spoken. He pointed behind her. Erin turned to see a hillside, rich with spring grass and dotted with prickly pear cactus topped with waxy yellow blossoms. Grazing cattle were ranged among them, standing as still as statues in the afternoon sun as they cropped slowly and meditatively at the grass.

"Do you know what those are?" he asked. When she didn't answer, he sighed and said, "Come on, hazard a guess."

Stung, she said, "Of course. They're cows."

"And over there?" His hand swept in the other direction, indicating a barn and a corral. "Those are horses. This is a working ranch. I raise cattle, which I can occasionally sell at a profit when the market isn't in the toilet. I also train horses. I need a good wrangler, or an experienced cowboy. Hell, I'd settle for someone who knows the head of a heifer from the rump. What I don't need is a butler."

Erin cleared her throat and kept her eyes steady on his. "Yes, well, Miss Eugenia said you'd be resistant."

His dark gaze pinned her. "Resistant doesn't begin to describe it," he said in a level tone. "Try bone-headed stubborn, which is the term she—and every other member of my family—usually uses."

Miss Eugenia had used exactly that phrase when she had described him and this job. Erin had hoped the dear lady was exaggerating.

Tyler went on, "I wouldn't let her cancel her South American cruise and stay with me so she decided to send you. A butler, for cryin' out loud. She knows that's the last thing I'd ever want around here. It brings to mind polished silver and finger sandwiches with the crusts cut off."

Erin blinked, taken aback at the preciseness of his description. It sounded quite personal, which surprised her even more.

Before she could think of anything to say, he

stopped and focused on her for a second. "What do your bosses call you? Miss Jones? Jonesy? Or do they go for the strictly utilitarian and call you Jones?"

Erin shook her head. She was having a hard time keeping up with him. "People aren't always so formal now. My employers usually call me Erin, or Miss Jones in front of guests."

"I'll bet they do," he scoffed. "Gotta keep up appearances no matter what. Although I have to say you're not the usual run-of-the-mill family retainer." Once again, his laughter cracked the air. "That's what I need around here, a butler who dyes her hair wild colors and rides a Honda through Mexico. I—" He broke off when the phone rang. He pivoted awkwardly on his crutch. "Where'd I leave the damned cordless phone? You stay right there," he snapped over his shoulder. "We'll clear this up and you can hightail it right back to my aunt and tell her to quit her meddling."

He slid the crutches backward and gave the door a shove with his elbow so that it shut with a snap right in her face.

TYLER MOVED with a shuffle-stomp through the living room. The pain that had been his unwelcome companion for a week intensified as his leg swung with the motion of the crutches. The break wasn't too bad. He'd had worse, but past experience had taught him that he was a fast healer. He'd had to spend a week in the hospital because the swelling was worse than he'd ever had before and the leg couldn't be casted until the swelling went down. During that time, he'd managed to fend off visits and concerned phone calls from his parents and Aunt Eugenia. He should have known his aunt would prevail.

He gritted his teeth against it, knowing he hadn't done himself any good by chasing Junior and Bucky around the house or by taking a tumble in the dirt thanks to Miss Erin Jones. Her guilty look at the dirt on his cast had told him she'd been responsible for his fall.

Hell, he should have stayed in the hospital, or in bed, he thought in frustration.

On the other hand, if he hadn't been so intent on escaping Shara's attempts at comforting and nursing him in his bedroom, he would never have gone to the kitchen for a beer and seen the two boys out the window. If he hadn't caught them when he did, he would be fighting a fire right now and trying to save the mares stabled in the barn—which would have done his leg a hell of a lot more damage then he was experiencing right now.

His gut clenched at the mental picture of what might have happened to his animals. He wished Earl Breslin would give up the rodeo circuit and come back to take care of his family. When he had moved Shara and the boys into the old Breslin family place across the road, he swore it was only temporary. He'd promised Shara he'd come home with big winnings and they'd move to Phoenix or Tucson, someplace with plenty of shopping malls where she could spend those big winnings.

Earl had also promised that if Tyler would look out for his family for a little while, he'd be back for them. All he had to do was win some of the big money.

Tyler still couldn't figure out how he'd ever fallen

for that line. He'd known Earl for ten years, and the man had never won big in any event he'd entered.

Now it had been almost a year since Shara and the boys had been across the road—and in Tyler's hair. She had begun talking about divorcing Earl. Unfortunately she did her talking in front of Junior and Bucky with the result that they'd become even more unruly than ever.

Sometimes Tyler thought God made Shara for only one reason and it wasn't for either motherhood or homemaking.

He wondered if Shara could use a butler. The idea almost made him laugh, though it wasn't as funny as the idea of Doris Jones's kid *being* a butler. He just couldn't picture her answering the door with a little bow from the waist, polishing silver, or organizing a garden party for two hundred people.

Tyler's leg throbbed again as he moved across the living room. It wasn't the first time he'd been on crutches, of course. During his rodeoing days he'd broken many bones. But in the two years since he'd used his winnings to buy this ranch, he'd led a relatively quiet life—until he'd been thrown and then stomped by a mare his neighbor's teenage son was trying to saddle break. The boy was new at it, and going about it all wrong, trying to force the mare rather than gentle her. Tyler had intervened, somehow getting between the horse and its owner. His broken leg was the result.

To top it off, the kid he'd been trying to help hadn't even come around to offer assistance with the chores while Tyler was in the hospital—the little twerp. Tyler was depending on another neighbor to help out.

He got into too many such situations; taking on lost causes; tilting at windmills. Shara and her sons were an example of his softheadedness. He'd be damned if he was going to add the Jones kid, too.

Grimacing, Tyler entered his small office on the far side of the living room and leaned against the edge of his desk as he grabbed the phone. His crutch clattered to the floor and he voiced a weary curse.

"Tyler, such language." Eugenia Morris's chiding tone rang clearly in his ear.

"Aunt Eugenia," he said grimly. "I think there's something you forgot to tell me...."

BACK ON THE PORCH, Erin stared with irritation at the door that had been slammed in her face. Miss Eugenia had said he was being released from the hospital and would probably hole up like a bear in its den. She hadn't warned Erin about his outright rudeness. Erin had no intention of waiting meekly outside until he came back. She had been hired to do a job, and she would do it. Grasping the doorknob with one hand and her suitcase with the other, she marched inside.

In the distance, she could hear Tyler's voice, sounding slightly less harsh, as he spoke to his caller.

She breathed out a long sigh, relieved that his ire had momentarily been turned from her and focused on some other undoubtedly innocent soul.

Eugenia had been right. This job was going to be *exactly* like moving into a bear's den with the bear still in residence.

Erin took another deep breath and stepped further into the house. "Might as well march right into the den," she murmured as her gaze darted around the

room. It looked as bad as Miss Eugenia had led her
to expect, with clothing, boots and newspapers scat-
tered around. Tyler had made himself a nest on a
sofa, but it didn't look very comfortable since the
sofa appeared to be several inches shorter than he
was.

For a moment, Erin's attention was pulled away
from the mess and caught by the room itself. She
studied it with pleased appreciation.

It was beautifully proportioned with walls painted
in fresh, stark white, an open beam ceiling, and
golden maple floors. There were framed prints by
Remington and Russell on the walls along with a
faded Navajo rug that took pride of place above the
cluttered brown leather sofa.

Erin stepped closer to examine it. This rug wasn't
one of those fake things sold in the parking lots of
corner gas stations. The worn spots told her it was
very old and no doubt genuine.

With new respect for the man who had chosen
such a piece, Erin surveyed the rest of the room.

A huge native fieldstone fireplace at the north end
was flanked by floor-to-ceiling windows that were
bare of any coverings. The room was very masculine
and utilitarian and made Erin feel as if she had
stepped back in time to the Old West. There was
even a gun cabinet built into one wall. It contained
several rifles and six-shooters. She gave it a nervous
glance, hoping it was locked. It was easy to imagine
Bucky and Earl Junior getting into it. She shuddered
at the thought and turned back to the room.

Through the windows she could see another field
of alfalfa and a row of Arizona cedars nearly twenty
feet tall. They bent and swayed in the breeze, giving

protection to a fruit orchard. Pink and white petals drifted from the newly budded peach and plum trees.

Erin gave the peaceful scene a wistful glance. Behind her, she could hear Tyler's carefully controlled voice as he spoke into the receiver. Erin set her suitcase down and walked to where she could hear him clearly. Mr. Westin would have been horrified by her nosiness. A good butler did *not* listen in on the employer's private conversations. She would have scrupulously observed that rule, but she had a hunch this conversation centered on her.

"Yes, Aunt Eugenia, she's here, but she won't be staying.... It's not the money.... No, you *won't* be taking care of her salary. She won't be earning a salary because she won't be staying." His voice grew very deep and purposeful. "I don't need a butler. I don't need a nursemaid." His voice dropped and softened as if he couldn't keep his affection for his aunt from slipping through. "I don't need interference from you or from Dad. I don't need anything."

Erin stepped around a pile of newspapers and walked to the doorway of the room where he was on the phone. It was his office. The space was filled with a desk topped by a computer, a beat-up file cabinet, and cases stuffed with books.

Tyler had shoved the computer keyboard to one side and propped himself on the edge of the desk. His casted leg stuck out before him at an awkward angle. When he glanced up, Erin noted with alarm that his face was gray with pain.

Mr. Westin said that every butler needed to know the time for retreat and the time for action—although he would be aghast if he saw what she was about to do. She strode across the room, her sensible shoes soundless on the wooden floor.

Reaching out, she said, "Allow me, sir." She took the receiver from his hand.

"Hey, wait..." he sputtered, grabbing for the phone, but she stepped back.

She gave her reluctant new employer a steady look while he frowned at her furiously. "I'm here, Miss Eugenia, and I'll be staying just as we discussed."

"Oh, thank goodness, I was afraid he would throw you out," Eugenia Morris said with a gusty sigh of relief.

Erin could picture her sitting in her pink and lavender living room worrying over her nephew. She was tiny and fluffy, but she had a will of iron. Obviously a family trait, Erin decided, glancing at her scowling employer. "No, that's not going to happen." She eyed the seething man before her and silently added *yet*.

"Then I feel comfortable going on my cruise. Let me speak to the dear boy again."

Calmly meeting Tyler's gaze, Erin handed the phone back to him. He growled into it and Eugenia's voice came clearly over the line, "Now, Tyler, don't try to intimidate Erin. She's a hard worker. She'll take good care of you. She's a delightful girl."

"Well, she can just go and be delightful somewhere else," he responded.

While his aunt continued with her exhortations, his gaze roamed over Erin again.

Erin fought to keep a blush from climbing her cheeks. She had been trained to be unobtrusive, to be present but invisible. The way Tyler was looking at her, she was present all right, and anything but invisible.

She could tell that at this moment, she wasn't a butler in his opinion. She was a woman—though not much of one. It was evident that he didn't like the look of her at all—though even he would have to admit it was a big improvement over the magenta dye job she'd had when last he'd seen her. Erin wondered if he preferred women like Shara of the tight red skirt.

He certainly looked as if he'd had better days—or months. She thought that he was probably a rugged-looking man at the best of times. Now, his face had a grayish cast, his high cheekbones stood in sharp relief to his long, straight nose and full lips. Erin found herself dwelling on those lips, then jerking her eyes away, uncomfortably aware of where her thoughts were heading. This was no time to start thinking of her employer as anything other than someone to serve.

After all, that's what she was being hired to do: to help an injured man. Eugenia had told her he'd been stomped by a neighbor's horse. Erin, who knew nothing about horses, couldn't imagine the horror of being attacked by an animal that weighed several hundred pounds. The damage to Tyler's leg was understandable. He would be laid up for weeks yet, maybe longer if he didn't take care of himself. In order to ease Miss Eugenia's worries, Erin was here to make sure he did.

She only wished that Miss Eugenia had been a little more specific about his stubbornness. Erin felt she should have been warned that the lovely, ladylike Miss Eugenia's nephew was a thoroughly unpleasant character. Even Erin's own mother, who had probably met him on a number of occasions, hadn't warned her.

Abruptly Tyler said goodbye to his aunt and hung up the phone. He fit the crutches under his arms. "It's time for you to go, Miss Jones. I'm sure you can find your way to the door."

"I'm staying," she answered calmly, though her heart quaked at the furious look he gave her. Erin cleared her throat and said firmly, "You heard me promise Miss Eugenia."

"I'm not responsible for your false promises. Let's get something straight here," he rapped out, extending his chin. "I don't like pushy women and I don't like interference." His ferocious scowl matched his tone.

And Erin didn't like stubborn, offensive men, but she could be stubborn, too, because she owed Miss Eugenia. "I understand that," she answered in a voice as tight as a stretched rubber band. "But Miss Eugenia is depending on me, and—"

"What Eugenia does with her money is her business...up to a point," he added. "But I don't need you here. I don't want you here, and I'm sure you can go home and collect your money from her while you sit around and file your nails."

Incensed, Erin hurried after him. "I have no intention of doing any such thing. I was hired to work for you and I intend to do it."

"I'll throw you out." The crutches battered the wooden floor angrily as he left the room.

Erin stomped along right behind him as he entered the living room. "Not until your leg is healed."

"If you think a broken leg will stop me, you're

wrong, sister.'' Tyler stopped suddenly, planted one crutch on the floor and started to pivot angrily toward her. Caught off guard, Erin barreled into him, knocking him sideways. His crutches crashed to the floor and Erin made a grab for him, but missed. She watched in horror as his hands shot out and he dove toward the floor. At the last second, he managed to lunge in the direction of the sofa and break his fall by landing against its edge. Still, he crumpled to the floor, with his left arm twisted under him.

''Oh, no, oh…Mr. Morris, are you all right?'' Erin fell to her knees beside him. Her hands hovered over him, but she didn't dare touch him.

Slowly Tyler turned his head to look at her. Pain and fury washed over his face. Through gritted teeth, he said, ''I'm having just a dandy day, thanks. I think you've broken my arm.''

ERIN SAT IN THE TINY FOYER of the hospital's emergency room and resisted the urge to lay her head down on her knees and weep.

Tyler had been wrong. His arm wasn't broken, only sprained badly enough that he wouldn't be able to use it for a couple of weeks. It had been swollen and purple by the time she had pulled into the emergency room entrance with him in the front seat of her car, swearing a blue streak, while her hastily contrived ice bag had dripped from his wrist and all over her upholstery.

Getting him out of the house and into her car had taken every bit of her strength. Holding her tongue through his furious diatribe, then his stony silence, had taken all her self-control. Even when he had called her a clumsy, meddling airhead, she had kept silent.

He was waiting now for the doctor to finish wrapping his arm and release him. Lucky her, she thought morosely, she could then take him home where she would be at the mercy of his surly temper once again. Too bad the hospital personnel wouldn't want to keep him, but they'd probably had a bellyful of him in the past week.

Erin rubbed her temples where a headache was beginning to pound and tried to decide at exactly what point things had started to go wrong.

It could have been when she had left her last job with Lord Vincent Mornfield. He had hired her right out of Mr. Westin's butler school. She had loved working in the Mornfield's London home, though the hours had been long and the schedule erratic. He and Lady Claudia had invited her to accompany them on their exploratory trek along the Orinoco River in South America, but she had declined because she hadn't thought she was cut out for the rugged life— her motorcycling and camping trek to Mexico years ago had taught her that.

Erin turned her head and sent a dark glance toward the small room where Tyler was being examined.

She had formed that opinion before she had met Tyler Morris, though. Now she realized she wouldn't have met anything along the Orinoco more intimidating than he was.

Maybe this whole thing had gone wrong when she had seen this job as a way of paying her debt to Miss Eugenia. The expensive butler school had been beyond her means, and it had been her mother's employer who had generously offered the funds to pay for it.

Erin grimaced. Why hadn't she been satisfied to go on paying Miss Morris in monthly increments? Oh, no, the opportunity had been offered and she'd wanted to take care of the entire debt in one swoop.

It was entirely because she had an overdeveloped fear of debt. There'd been so little money around while her mother had been raising Erin and her three brothers that they'd all harbored fears some tragedy would befall them if they didn't keep every bill paid exactly on time.

In spite of Tyler's suggestion that she should go home and file her nails while collecting a salary, there was no real salary involved. She planned to live frugally on her savings for the duration of her service with Tyler, collecting no pay. According to her agreement with Miss Eugenia, her debt would be paid when Tyler no longer needed her.

She reached up to rub her temples. From the looks of things, that would happen about five minutes after she got Tyler back home.

Erin slumped down in the chair and kicked off her shoes, giving up the appearance of perfect correctness she'd been trying to maintain. Correctness, or even comfort, was impossible in this chair, anyway. Its rounded plastic back had been designed by some opportunist hoping to drum up business for the nearest chiropractor.

If Tyler let her stay, she was well and truly going to be earning her debt-free state now. She might have to stay with him even longer than she had planned, especially now that she had been the cause of further misfortune for him. The month to six weeks she had allotted to this job could stretch out indefinitely.

The quiet swish of a wheelchair drew her attention and she hastily slipped her feet back into her shoes as she turned to see a harried-looking nurse wheeling Tyler into the waiting room.

His wrist was tightly wrapped and his arm was in a sling. His face held a scowl that would have stopped a charging rhino.

"He's signed the insurance papers and he's all ready to go," the nurse chirped. The forced cheerfulness in her voice couldn't disguise the relieved look in her eyes at the realization that Erin was going to take Tyler away. No doubt, he'd been turning on the charm.   "He's going to have to use the wheelchair for a few days, though—at least until his wrist is strong enough to hold him up on the crutches," the woman added, then turned to Tyler. "Aren't you lucky you had a friend available to bring you in?"

Tyler tilted his head back and glared through narrowed eyes. "She's no friend of mine," he growled.

Erin stiffened her spine and ignored the sting those words caused. "That's right," she said briskly. "I'm his butler." Turning away from the puzzled nurse and her scowling patient, she continued, "I'll bring the car around."

By the time she had driven to the bottom of the ramp outside the emergency room, the nurse had rolled Tyler out. Erin opened the car door, and then the trunk. Efficiently, she helped Tyler into the car, stowed the wheelchair in the trunk, then thanked the nurse who waved them away saying, "Good luck." She quietly added, "You'll need it."

Erin didn't doubt that for a second. Tyler maintained his stony silence throughout the ride back to his ranch. Erin didn't say anything, either. After all, what *could* she say? ''Sorry, I knocked you down and sprained your wrist? But if I promise not to do it again, could I please stay and work off my debt to your aunt?''

When they reached the house, Erin had only a moment to ponder the problem of getting the wheelchair up the stairs. Tyler solved it by slipping from the car onto the ground, then scooting backward up the short sidewalk and the stairs. It took time because he couldn't use his left hand, but Erin didn't dare offer help. When he was on the porch, she followed with the wheelchair.

As he pulled himself into the chair using his one good arm and leg, Erin surveyed the wide sweep of the porch and said, ''You know, it wouldn't be very much trouble to install a ramp here.''

''Why?'' Tyler asked in a stoical tone. ''Once you're gone, I probably won't need it. Do you intend to stick around to see how much more damage you can do?''

''I intend to stick around,'' Erin answered frostily as she took his key and unlocked the front door. ''I promised Miss Eugenia.'' Grasping the handles of the chair, she swept him inside. ''The nurse said you already have some pain pills. You need to take one and go right to bed. I'll fix you something to eat.''

Tyler grasped the wheel rim with his good hand and swung himself around to face her. Erin's hands sprang away and she stepped back in surprise. His voice was as grim as the lines carved into his face. ''I'm not taking those damned pills,'' he said in a low, threatening tone. ''*I* will decide when I need to go to bed. *I* will fix myself something to eat and *you* will take your suitcase and leave.''

Erin bit back furious words. "Mr. Morris, I thought we had already established that. I have to stay because Miss Eugenia is depending on me.''

"Well, I won't tell her if you won't. Just leave, Miss Jones," he said wearily. "Before you cause more trouble.''

Though he was being completely unfair, Erin once again kept her thoughts to herself—something she was finding increasingly hard to do.

With her jaw set as stubbornly as his, Erin pushed the wheelchair toward the hallway where the bedrooms were. She was moving along slowly, when Tyler shot his hand out and grabbed one wheel rim. "In here," he said, swinging the chair around.

Erin couldn't stop her forward momentum in time to keep from running the chair into the door frame.

Tyler groaned in pain, then said, testily, "In the short time you've been here, I've gone from crutches to a wheelchair. Are you trying for a stretcher next, or a casket?''

Although she wanted to tell him she was hoping for both, she answered "Neither," in a tone that matched his. Then she added, "I'm sorry.''

He snorted derisively as she backed the chair up and made the turn into his room.

Her sweeping glance took in the old-fashioned iron bed frame, painted white, the dark blue quilt that topped the high mattress, masses of pillows and the braided rug on the floor.

Either Tyler hadn't used this room since his return from the hospital, or someone had cleaned up in here. As soon as the thought formed, she glanced around again, then her eyes widened and she stopped in her tracks. Her anger at Tyler faded into surprise.

Along with the distinctively masculine furnishings, there were vases of flowers, arrangements of scented candles and dishes of potpourri. The shades were pulled against the afternoon sun, making the room dark and intimate.

The place reeked of seduction.

3

SHE MUST HAVE STOOD STILL too long because Tyler twisted around in his chair and glared at her. She couldn't keep the question out of her eyes when they met his.

"Shara," he snapped, his expression defying her to say anything more.

What could she say except, "Oh?" and resist the urge to add a comment about the woman being either an opportunist or an optimist. Of course, there was always the possibility that Tyler and Shara frequently shared a bed. Earl Junior seemed to think that Tyler was going to be his new father.

A very long silence followed in which she tried to remember something, *anything,* James Westin had told her about getting out of an embarrassing situation. She knew what to do if she happened to find her employer in bed with a partner—don't speak unless spoken to by the guest. She even knew how to get rid of an unwelcome caller—phone for a cab right away and escort the departing visitor to the door. She even knew that when she spoke, she was supposed to pitch her voice a bit lower than the other person in the conversation. But this scenario wasn't one for which she had been prepared.

Best to say nothing, James would have advised. Erin cleared her throat, then continued in her most matter-of-fact tone, "Would you like some assistance into bed?"

Tyler's glare froze momentarily. As she watched, his eyes, so dark the pupils were almost indistinguishable, seemed to lighten. "I don't need your help into bed, Miss Jones," he said in a silky growl. "I've been managing to get myself, and anyone who wants to come with me, there on my own for years."

Heat washed beneath Erin's skin and she prayed that it didn't show. A new tactic, she decided. If he couldn't insult her enough to drive her away, he wasn't above trying sexual innuendos. Erin held onto her temper with an effort. As long as it didn't turn into sexual harassment, she could deal with this.

"Fine," she answered coolly as she lifted her hands from the wheelchair handles and turned to leave the room. "Then it goes without saying that you won't need assistance in the bathroom, either." Even as she said it, Erin didn't know how he was going to even *enter* the bathroom, much less use the facilities there, but *she* wasn't going to be the one to offer to help him—not if she would like to keep her head attached to her shoulders. "I'll go fix you something to eat."

"I told you I don't want you to. Shara said she brought some homemade chicken soup. I'll have that and I can get it myself."

Erin didn't pause, but kept right on walking down the hall, across the living room and into the kitchen as she told herself that she wasn't going to let his bad temper get to her. She had a job to do, a debt to pay, and she was going to pay it no matter how tough, how verbally abusive, her new employer became.

The kitchen turned out to be a large, old-fashioned room that looked out to the backyard. It had faded gray linoleum on the floor and cabinets that had been painted avocado green, presumably during the 1970s, and never touched again. Where the paint wasn't streaked and faded, it was cracked and chipped. Erin concluded that modernizing the kitchen simply wasn't one of Tyler's priorities.

Neither was cleaning it. Erin grimaced when she saw that dirty dishes were piled in the sink and across the white-tiled counters. On the stove sat an empty pot, obviously the one Shara had set out to use for her "homemade" soup. Beside it was a familiar red-and-white can whose contents were advertised as being "M'm! M'm! Good."

Erin snickered, removed her jacket and rolled up her sleeves. "Homemade soup, hmm? I'll show him some homemade soup."

She was gratified to see that the cupboards and the refrigerator were well stocked. She found a package of fresh chicken, put it on to cook, then whipped out eggs and flour, checking closely for staleness and weevils, and made a batch of noodles. While the soup simmered, she made biscuits, slipped them into the oven and went in search of a tray.

For a moment, she considered slapping the food onto the tray, carrying it in and thumping it down in front of him, but James Westin's very expensive training wouldn't let her be so careless. After several minutes of digging through drawers and cupboards, she found a couple of cloth napkins. Though it pained her sense of rightness to see that they were mismatched, she folded one into a fan and placed it in the soup bowl. She used the other one to line the tray.

Tucked into the back of a cabinet, she found a small bud vase into which she slipped a sprig cut from the small lilac bush struggling to grow beside the front steps.

As she worked, she thought about Tyler Morris. Miss Eugenia had warned her about his black mood. He didn't like being laid up, didn't like having to depend on other people. Erin could understand that because she valued her independence, too. What puzzled her was his violent objections to having her here. In spite of his taunts about her wild past, she didn't think that was why he didn't want her around. He didn't seem to be a judgmental person and if they were going to compare wild pasts, hers was mild compared to his.

There was more to his attitude than that, but she didn't know what. Miss Eugenia had been sketchy about information concerning Tyler, and Erin now suspected that it had been deliberate.

Really, all she knew was that he'd never been married and his only relatives were his parents, who lived in Phoenix, and Miss Eugenia in Tucson.

Erin, one of four children and part of a large extended family of aunts, uncles and cousins couldn't imagine having such a paltry number of family members. In spite of the size and closeness of her family, she couldn't help envying Tyler one thing—his father was still alive. Erin's had abandoned the family when she was five and died somewhere in California a few years later. She couldn't remember a thing about him.

An hour after she had left Tyler alone, Erin rolled

down the sleeves of her blouse, replaced her jacket and reentered the bedroom carrying the nicely arranged tray. Tyler didn't possess any such thing as a soup tureen, so she'd put it in a small saucepan for serving. Though she was ever critical of her own work, Erin had the satisfaction of knowing the meal tasted as good as it looked and smelled, and that even James Westin himself could find no fault with the setting.

As she walked in, with her thumbs placed correctly along the lip of the tray and not lapping over the top, she glanced up and saw that Tyler had indeed made it from the wheelchair to the bed. He lay sprawled across the quilt, his injured arm and leg held out from his body at awkward angles. In spite of the discomfort his position must be causing him, he appeared to be asleep.

Holding the tray against her hip, Erin quietly cleared Shara's candles and potpourri dishes off the bedside table to make room for the food. As she did, she couldn't help wondering again if there was some kind of relationship between Tyler and Shara. He hadn't seemed happy with her presence that day, or with that of her sons, but then, he hadn't been in the best of moods and Erin thought it may have been the pain talking. After she finished clearing the table, she set down the tray of food.

Tyler didn't wake and she wondered if he had finally given in and taken one of the pain pills the doctor had prescribed, or if he was simply so exhausted he'd fallen asleep in spite of the pain.

She should wake him, get him to eat and then make him more comfortable on the bed. She knew exactly how to position a pillow under his leg to relieve pressure on his hip joint. Erin reached out to him, then paused and let her hand drop back to her side as she studied him.

Even in sleep, he didn't seem to relax, though she knew the frown that creased his brow might also be the result of pain rather than the anger and irritation that had so far been his only expressions.

Erin realized with a start that he was younger than she had thought at first. His thick hair, as rich as dark chocolate, was barely touched by gray, but his face had the beginning of lines and seams that were the result of years in the sun and of the intense focus he seemed to bring to whatever he did. Later, those lines and seams would deepen into creases that would only add to his craggy attractiveness.

Though he was tall enough to stretch almost the length of the bed, Tyler was lithe and sinewy rather than brawny. His shoulders were broad but not bulky, the muscles long and lean beneath the skin. She knew that they had developed from years of hard use, not sculpted in the local health club or gym.

Looking at him, at the latent strength and power in his sleeping form, Erin felt a twinge of awareness spark through her. Her eyes widened in surprise at herself and she glanced away. She was no blushing innocent, for goodness' sake and she'd been raised with three brothers. They'd wandered around the house in their Skivvies her whole life so she certainly was no stranger to what a man's body looked like.

Erin took a breath to cool the heat that was spiraling through her and pressed her palms together as she acknowledged the truth: none of her short, stocky brothers looked like this.

Erin told herself that this certainly wasn't a professional way to behave. James would choke in outrage if he knew she was standing in her employer's bedroom, ogling him, something she'd certainly never been tempted to do with plump and balding Lord Vincent Mornfield—even if Lady Claudia would have allowed it.

Deliberately she dragged her attention away, but it came right back to Tyler.

No doubt his body type and strength had been assets to him when he'd been on the rodeo circuit. Miss Eugenia had proudly recounted his triumphs, even while she admitted that she had been mystified as to why he wanted to pursue such a dangerous sport.

Erin had known him less than four hours, but she guessed that he probably had an adventurous nature that had fed on the danger and challenge of the rodeo events. She saw many scars on his hands and arms. One showed on his elbow, a white streak against the tan skin and she wondered if it had been broken there and had required surgery.

All in all, he looked like a man whose body had been well used, and abused, as he had pursued his goals.

Erin frowned, unable to understand that kind of determination. It was true that she had done daring things in the not-so-distant past, such as riding alone across Mexico on a Honda, but she had never deliberately set out on a course of action that was almost certain to bring her bodily harm.

Now, she smiled when she thought about that time, the most rebellious of her life. She couldn't remember exactly what she'd been rebelling against, except perhaps her mother's work ethic, which had surfaced in her after all.

She'd had a number of jobs, mostly as a salesclerk, before it had occurred to her that she much preferred working in the back room to dealing with customers. Taking inventory and straightening the stock gave her a feeling of satisfaction that sales didn't provide. Eventually she'd reached the conclusion that what she really liked was clearing up messes, organizing things and performing the nice little everyday ceremonies that made life pleasant. When she'd heard about James Westin's butler school in London, she'd known it was the place for her. Too bad someone like Tyler Morris couldn't appreciate all her training.

Erin's gaze traveled over him, from the open neck of his shirt, over his chin and his straight nose. A slight smile curved her lips as she speculated that his nose might be the only part of his body he hadn't broken or bruised at some point and she wondered how it had escaped the battering the rest of his body had endured.

Lost as she was in her thoughts, it was a couple of seconds before Erin realized that Tyler's eyes were open and staring into hers.

"Oh...you're awake."

Tyler watched a flush of color run beneath Erin's skin and stain her cheeks. For the first time in three weeks, he felt a genuine smile coming on. The contrasts in her amused him. Before today, he hadn't seen her for at least six years, but he'd never forgotten his only sight of Doris Jones's wild daughter.

The last time he had seen her, he had smiled at his Aunt Eugenia's description of her escapades even as he had admired her nerve. That same reckless streak ran through him; maybe dormant now because he was in business for himself so he couldn't allow himself to take chances, but the recklessness was still there.

This girl had not only lost her wild streak, but she had turned into a combination of Jeeves and Mary Poppins. He was interested to see that there was something else thrown in, too. Just now she had been staring at him in a way that a man recognized as more than passing interest.

That surprised the hell out of him considering how he had treated her all day.

Erin cleared her throat and he wondered if she was berating herself for behaving as if she were a stammering adolescent girl caught peeking at a skin magazine.

No reason to make things easy for her, he decided. Once she got a load of the real work around this place, she would be gone soon enough.

"And you're still here," he answered in a sleep-roughened voice.

He could see her grit her teeth. "I've made you some dinner." She indicated the tray.

He groaned, imagining the soup that Shara had left. In spite of what he had said to Erin, he'd hoped that either he wouldn't have to eat it at all, or that it would be of the canned variety. Shara was a lousy cook.

Tyler raised himself on one elbow, mentally cursed the pain that shot up from his right leg and his left wrist and glanced over as she lifted a kitchen towel off the tray and folded it carefully corner to corner as she watched for his reaction.

His face went blank with surprise as he examined a steaming pot of soup that didn't look like anything Shara could have produced out of ability or out of a can. There was also a neat stack of flaky biscuits, butter cut into precise pats and a bud vase with a lilac sprig. Tyler blinked.

"What's the matter?" Erin asked.

"Hmph. I didn't even know I *owned* a bud vase. If I had, I probably would have tossed it out."

"Why?" Surprise rang in her voice.

"Because they're nothing but dust collectors. I bought this place and most of the furnishings 'as is' when the previous owner died. I got rid of most of the clutter, but it looks like there's still stuff that needs to be tossed."

Her eyebrows rose and he couldn't hide the grin that kicked up one corner of his mouth. "I bet you flunked the class on mastery of the deadpan expression in butler school, Miss Jones." He pulled himself to a sitting position. "I know what you're thinking."

"Do you now?" She folded her hands at her waist and he had to admit that it was quite an efficient little gesture.

"You're wondering why a man who lives in a place that looks like a pigsty would object to a few dust collectors."

"Well," she answered judiciously. "I wouldn't exactly call this place a pigsty, but I'm wondering why you would object to a bud vase."

"Let's just say it's a long-standing prejudice." Tyler glanced once again at the food. If it tasted as good as it smelled, he could probably swallow it in one gulp. "Shara didn't make that."

"No, I did."

Tyler looked at her calm expression and had to admire her nerve, which, apparently, she hadn't lost, after all. He had tried to throw her out several times, but she hadn't gone. He liked that kind of moxie. On the other hand, if she had gone, he probably wouldn't have a sprained wrist now. He could refuse to eat it, but he was hungry. Boneheaded he might be, but he wasn't stupid.

"Looks great." With his good hand, he reached for the tray.

Erin was so surprised by his sudden change in attitude that she started, made a grab for the tray at the same moment he did and nearly upset it in his lap.

"Oh, sorry," she said. Flustered, she shook out the napkin to spread over his lap.

With an appalled look, he snatched it away. "I can do that myself," he grumped. "Quit fussing over me."

Frustrated, Erin reached for the soup ladle, but even serving that was denied her when he grabbed it from her hand. "Next you'll be trying to feed me."

"Not if I want to keep all my fingers attached to my hand," she muttered.

Tyler glanced up sharply. "Ah," he said with satisfaction. "The polished veneer has a crack."

Erin straightened and gave him her most superior look. "Will there be anything else, sir?"

He winced. "Yeah, don't call me sir—Jonesy."

That set Erin's teeth on edge, but she didn't respond for fear of fracturing their fragile truce. "I'll return for the tray in a little while."

"And bring about six more biscuits with you," he instructed, devouring his first in two bites.

With a nod, Erin returned to the kitchen. She hated to deal in stereotypes, but perhaps it was true that the way to a man's heart was through his stomach. She stopped and frowned. Not that she was interested in appealing to his heart. She would simply like to get through the next few weeks without coming to blows with him.

As he had requested, Erin took him some more biscuits and left him alone to eat them.

On her way back to the kitchen for her own long-delayed dinner, she almost let her shoulders slump in dismay when she heard footsteps on the porch, then a knock on the door. Would the surprises never end around here? Straightening, she walked to the front of the house.

She opened the door to find a tall, thin cowboy who whipped off his hat as soon as he saw Erin. The porch light revealed his balding head, friendly, gap-toothed grin and pleasantly homely face. "Excuse me, ma'am," he said, examining her with deep curiosity. "Is Ty here?"

"Yes, he is. Won't you come in?" She stepped back so he could enter. Meticulously he wiped his feet as he looked around with interest, then back at her.

"May I ask who is calling, please?" Erin asked.

A puzzled frown clouded his face for a moment, then cleared. "Calling? Oh, oh, I get it." He nodded and grinned as if she had cracked a good joke. He finished wiping his feet as he said, "Tell him Sam Wettig's here. I'm a neighbor—been helping out since he got hurt and his hired hand quit." He paused and looked her over with appreciation in his blue eyes. "You his new lady? I been tellin' him he needed to get a good woman, not someone like that crazy she-cat, Shara. I never saw you around here before."

"I only arrived today...."

"Oh? Did you two just meet? He's a damned fast worker, what with his broken leg and all. What's your name, honey?"

The blood rushed to Erin's cheeks. "No," she said quickly. "I'm not his lady. I'm his butler and my name is Erin Jones."

Sam looked at her for a moment as if he was trying to decide if she was joking. Apparently she was because he reached out with a hand as big as a Virginia ham and gave her a clap on the shoulder that nearly sent her to her knees. "And quite a little kidder, too," he said with a loud laugh. "Where is that sly dog?"

Erin flexed her shoulder and hoped it wasn't broken. "In the bedroom."

Sam started off in that direction, then rocked to a stop. He glanced at her with a comically bashful look. "Oh, uh, hey, I'm sorry. I didn't mean to interrupt anything important."

Erin looked up at the distressed cowboy and wondered what on earth was going on inside that bald head. "Don't worry, you didn't interrupt anything. Go on in."

This time, he was the one to blush as he headed for Tyler's bedroom. Rolling her eyes, Erin followed. The proper thing would have been for her to go ahead and announce him, but after less than half a day in this house, she had pretty much given up on any notion of doing anything in the expected way. It was too bad, too, she thought as she followed the long-legged visitor. Doing things in a proper and classy manner was what she liked best about her job.

She reached the bedroom just as Sam was saying, "Well, hell, Ty, what have you done to yourself now?'' He pulled up a chair, spun it around backward so he could straddle it and place his arms along the top of the back and prepared to listen.

Since she didn't want to hear what Tyler had to say about his sprained wrist, she went into the kitchen to make coffee. She returned with it in time to hear Sam discussing the work he had done around the ranch. He said, ''I looked on the north side of the mesa and couldn't find more than ten head. I thought you said there were at least thirty there.''

Tyler pushed his tray away and half turned toward Sam. ''There are. I drove them up there myself not two weeks ago. Diamond Creek is full from the rain we've had so I thought they'd be all right there for a while. Is there a fence down?''

''Nuh-uh. I'll look for them again tomorrow, though. They gotta be somewhere.''

Tyler nodded, but Erin noticed that he didn't seem as sure as Sam did. He stared absently at the quilt as Sam looked up to see Erin entering with the coffee. The tall cowboy gratefully accepted a cup and added and stirred four teaspoons of sugar into it. At the same time, he was giving a close examination to Erin's gray pin-striped suit.

Sam took a gulp of coffee, blotted his mouth with the back of his hand and said, ''Did somebody die?''

''Not yet,'' Tyler said darkly as he accepted a cup from Erin.

Erin suspected that threat was directed at her, but she ignored it as she had done most things he had said today. ''This is my uniform.''

Sam's face cleared. ''Oh,'' he burst out. ''You work for an airline.''

''No, I work for Mr. Morris.''

"It was my aunt Eugenia's idea," Tyler murmured into his cup.

Erin gave him a startled look. She had expected him to tell Sam that he was going to toss her out as soon as she finished washing the dishes.

Tyler met her eyes and they widened fractionally as if he knew what she was thinking and was secretly laughing at her.

Was it possible that he was teasing her or softening toward her, or—most unimaginable—that he had a sense of humor?

Sam didn't seem to have heard either of them or noticed their silent byplay. His homely face had taken on a dreamy expression. "You two gonna get married, Ty? You want me to be your best man? I was best man for Earl and Shara." He looked disgruntled. "The way things have turned out with them don't mean I didn't do a good job as best man. I didn't lose the ring or nothin'. But I hope your wedding can wait till I get a chance to go to Tucson. I got a good suit, but I need some new boots."

Stunned, Erin stared at him, unable to answer. Tyler's lips twitched as he said, "We haven't planned that far ahead, Sam."

Erin started to squeak out a protest but Sam broke in. "Better not leave it too late, buddy. You're not gettin' any younger."

"We'll remember that," Tyler said solemnly. "And we'll let you know when we set the date."

"Fair enough." Sam stood, handed his cup back to Erin and bobbed his head politely. "Fine coffee, ma'am. I wish I could stay, but somebody's comin' to weld me a new trailer hitch tonight. You want me to take care of the chores for you, Ty?"

"No. I've got it covered," Tyler answered.

With a wave, Sam ambled out the door and down the hallway.

Erin, whose good manners and training had been thrown into chaos by Sam's questions, could only stare after him.

She heard Tyler chuckling and turned wide eyes on him. "Maybe you'd better get while the getting's good," he advised. "Or Sam will have us married and be picking out baby names before you know it."

Erin swallowed. "He's very...imaginative, isn't he?"

"He's an ex-rodeo clown who got kicked in the head by a bull. Somehow that filled him with all kinds of romantic notions—for himself and for everyone else. Trouble is, he hasn't met the right woman yet."

Erin speculated that was because the ones he met realized very quickly that he'd been kicked in the head by a bull.

"He thinks you and I are getting married—and you let him think that!"

Now Tyler was openly grinning at her. "Why spoil his romantic notions?"

"Because they're wrong?" she suggested, scooping up the coffee tray. She heard Tyler chuckle as she returned it to the kitchen.

She should have been irritated, she concluded as she dipped out a bowl of soup for herself and picked up a couple of biscuits. But she knew from a lifetime of dealing with males, that if they were teasing her they weren't angry. She hoped that it was a further sign that he was softening toward the idea of letting her stay.

Erin smiled to herself. She had learned one new thing: Tyler Morris had a great smile.

As she ate, Erin cautiously congratulated herself on the way things were turning out. Though it wasn't the way she had expected, she prided herself on being flexible. Perhaps Tyler was still intent on having her leave, but if he was beginning to accept her just a bit, she could use that to her advantage. Besides, she could prepare any number of arguments to avoid leaving. She was convinced that she could overcome each obstacle by dealing with it calmly and rationally.

With renewed confidence, she washed the dishes quickly and headed back to the bedroom to see if Tyler needed anything. She found him sitting on the side of the bed, reaching for his crutches.

She skidded to a stop in the doorway. "What are you doing?"

He didn't look up as he answered. "I have stock to tend to in the barn."

Erin gaped at him. "You can't even use those crutches because of your wrist. How do you expect to be able to tend stock?"

"Same way I've always done, only slower."

Erin's determination to be calm and rational flew right out the window. She threw her hands in the air. "Oh, for goodness' sake. You can't possibly do your chores."

Tyler sat back and viewed her cynically. "Why, exactly, are you here?"

"I told you, to assist you."

"In any way?"

Erin's green eyes narrowed. "Well, within reason," she hedged.

"Then you can feed the stock."

She should have said yes, or that she would be happy to. What blurted from her mouth was, "You've got to be kidding."

"What's the matter? This butlering job getting to be too hard for you?"

Not hard. Impossible.

Erin lifted her chin. "Certainly not. It's just that I've never even been close to a horse."

"Then I'll have to tell you what to do," he responded in a silky voice.

Erin watched as Tyler tried to stand and balance himself, but he fell backward onto the bed, his casted leg sticking out awkwardly and his wrapped wrist flying into the air. He cursed through his teeth and tried again.

"Oh, all right then," Erin exploded. "I'll take you out in the wheelchair and you can tell me what to do."

Tyler looked as if he wanted to argue, which wouldn't have surprised Erin at all, but instead he nodded. "That'll work."

Within a few minutes, Erin had helped him into the chair, maneuvered it through the house, down the back stairs and across the yard to the barn. Inside, he told her where to find feed and grain for the horses, and how to throw down a supply of hay.

As she worked, Erin stepped carefully around the piles of horse manure on the barn floor. If she stayed, she had a pretty good idea who would be cleaning up those piles.

The horses intimidated her. She couldn't recall ever being this close to one before—and she was none too sure she wanted to be this close now. With a quick, sideways glance, she looked to see if Tyler was watching her. He was, no doubt to make sure she didn't harm his animals.

Considering all they'd been through today, she could understand that. They were probably valuable. She, on the other hand, was free.

Moving cautiously, she checked the grain supplies as Tyler directed and closed and locked the small back door. She thought that was a precaution to keep Junior and Bucky out, but she wasn't sure it would do much good. From what she had seen, they could pick just about any lock.

By the time she was finished, it was after eight o'clock and she was exhausted. Even Tyler looked as if he couldn't muster up much of an argument if she took him back inside and insisted he go to bed.

As they were leaving the barn, Erin heard a rustling noise near the door. Remembering that Junior and Bucky had been intent on playing with the baby kittens, she left Tyler sitting in the wheelchair and walked over to take a peek.

"If you're looking for Sheba's kittens, she won't let you near them," Tyler advised. "Better stay away."

"I'm only going to look at them," Erin answered. "Maybe Sheba would like some milk."

"She'd like to be left alone," he answered, his tone implying that Sheba wasn't the only one.

Erin looked over her shoulder. "If you can trust me to feed your horses, you can trust me to do no harm to your cats."

"Suit yourself."

Erin heard the rustling sound again and saw a flash of black-and-white disappear behind a pile of straw inside one of the stalls. On tiptoe, she approached the stall and reached down carefully to sift through the pile. It wasn't Sheba the barn cat and her new brood of cuddly kittens that she found, however.

It was a skunk.

4

ERIN SHRIEKED, tossed her hard-won dignity to the four winds and stumbled back, falling against Tyler.

"Hey!" he yelled. "Watch out. What the...?"

"A skunk!" Erin's scream split the air as she turned, scrambling to get away. She barely had wits enough to grab for the handles of the wheelchair in an attempt to take him and it along with her as she fled.

"Shut up," Tyler hissed as he rocked from one side of the chair to the other. "Or it will..."

Tyler's warning came too late. The startled skunk defended itself in the way nature had intended: by lifting its tail and spraying its noxious mess over them. Erin tried to twist away, but she stumbled over Tyler and got the worst of it on her behind.

She screeched as she felt the toxic wetness hit her clothes and skin. It landed with the force of a bomb.

Tyler's uninjured arm shot out to grab her as she lurched into him. He grunted in pain and folded over to the side when she banged his leg. This allowed the skunk's spray to lace his exposed arm, but with less force because Erin had already received the brunt of it.

Having safeguarded its life from the marauding human, the skunk turned toward the open barn door and scuttled away, its fluffy black-and-white tail raised as a banner of triumph.

Erin, slumped over Tyler, could only stare as the disappearing victor abandoned the field of battle, its backside waddling smugly into the night.

"Oh, my God," she groaned in horror. The stench of skunk permeated her clothing and hair, making her stomach roll and pitch. The chicken soup and biscuits she'd eaten threatened to put in a second appearance. She gagged, choked and pinched her nose, but it did no good against the overpowering smell. It seemed to have soaked instantly into the very core of her being.

"Aaargh," she groaned again, unable to form words strong enough to describe her dismay.

"Erin," Tyler pleaded in a strangled voice. "Get off me."

Dazed, she looked down at him. Her left arm was pressed against his windpipe. Her breast was almost in his eye. He looked as sick and horrified as she felt. She pushed away from him and staggered to her feet. The motion sent a wave of the stench wafting around them and she gripped her nose again.

"Are you all right?" Tyler asked in a strangled voice.

"Whad do you dink?" Erin asked, her fingers pinching for all they were worth. The gesture was pointless because she could still taste it. She knew she was going to be sick any second now.

"I think you've gotten us into a hell of a mess here." Tyler choked out the words. He started to lift his hand to rub his throat, then gasped harshly at the smell, and let his arm dangle beside the chair.

Erin dropped her hands to her sides, but when they

touched dampness, she jerked them away again in revulsion. Standing hunched over, arms out, feet apart, she looked up at him, her white face miserable.

"It was a skunk," she announced unnecessarily.

"No kidding. I told you to leave...."

Tears spurted into her eyes and she lifted a shaking finger to point at him. "Don't you dare say, 'I told you so'!"

"It's not necessary," he muttered. "I think you've learned your lesson—if I'm lucky," he added. Then his voice hardened as he looked at her face. "Don't faint and don't throw up," he commanded.

Erin gave him a furious look. As if things weren't bad enough, he was still tossing out orders.

"I wouldn't give you the satisfaction," she snapped back, but the breath she drew in when she said it brought another wave of the putrid odor and she gagged again. She didn't know if she could keep that promise.

Behind them, the horses were growing restive, shuffling in their stalls, and snorting. One of the mares tossed her head and screamed in fear at the loathsome odor.

Tyler glanced around. "We've got to get out of here. This is scaring the horses."

"Well, I'm not exactly enjoying it myself."

Tyler gave her a glance that said she shouldn't be complaining since she was the one who had caused the problem.

Erin was wise enough to close her mouth, wrap her palms around the handles of the wheelchair and follow the path that the skunk had already taken into the fresh air. Once they reached the yard, the stench dissipated a bit, but not enough to help the nausea that heaved her stomach back and forth.

"We can't go into the house," Tyler said as she stopped at the bottom of the back steps. "At least not until you've had a bath."

"A bath?" Erin gave him a stupefied look. "All the bath soap in the world won't help this smell."

"You've got that one right," he groused.

"Besides, maybe you've forgotten, but the bathrooms are inside the house."

Tyler tilted his head back and squinted at her through the evening gloom. "How do you think people took baths before indoor bathrooms?"

"With great difficulty!"

"In a washtub. There's a galvanized metal one on a hook in the tack room. I use it for washing down the animals. There's a bucket, too. Go get them, but bring me the cordless phone, first. I'm going to have to call someone to help us."

"We're beyond help," she insisted, but she didn't expect a response. Though she didn't want to take the smell into the house, she knew it was already there. Sick and disoriented, she staggered up the steps to begin the search for the telephone.

"Make it fast."

Erin tossed a furious look over her shoulder and stomped into the house. Did he think she was going to stop and give herself a manicure along the way? Or find the phone and call up a few girlfriends to laugh over what had happened?

Tyler caught the fury in her face. With a rueful shake of his head, he grudgingly admired her for her spunk. As long as she was mad, she would keep going, but he had the feeling she might fall apart if she stopped being angry with him and gave herself a minute to think about the situation.

Hell, they both knew that if she'd listened to him this wouldn't have happened, but there was no point in belaboring that.

He'd almost asked if such occasions hadn't been covered in butler school, but even he wasn't that cruel. He'd been a bastard to her all day, but he had his limits.

He looked down at the arm that had been sprayed. He grimaced and jerked his head away. He had a strong stomach, but not that strong.

Reaching up, he jerked the sleeve out of the arm-hole. Stitches popped and fabric ripped as it came away. He'd ruined the shirt, but it had been ruined anyway and there was no point in letting the poison soak in any further. He tossed the fabric onto the ground and turned his head away from the stench. His gaze fell on his uninjured leg and he wondered fatalistically if anything could happen to it. As of this afternoon, he was a true believer in the saying that if things can get worse, they probably will.

At that moment, Erin stalked out of the house, pounded down the steps and tossed the cordless phone into his lap. "Will there be anything else, sir?" she snapped.

"Yeah," he drawled. "The washtub and bucket."

Whipping around, she strode away, the skirt of her proper little uniform flapping wetly around her knees.

She stopped and glanced back at him. "Who are you going to call?"

"Skunkbusters," he deadpanned.

Her lips thinned. She didn't appreciate his feeble joke.

''Shara,'' he sighed. ''She'll have plenty to say about this. There'll be hell to pay, but there's been hell to pay since you walked into my life this afternoon. A little more won't matter.''

''No, it probably won't,'' Erin answered. Turning, she stomped away.

Tyler felt a twinge of guilt as he watched her go, but not enough to apologize. If she'd minded her own business, none of this would have happened. Savagely he squinted at the phone pad and punched out Shara's number.

''LADY, YOU STINK.''

Erin lifted her head from her knees when she heard the gruff little voice. She was seated on a patch of grass, her foul smelling skirt pulled down over her knees, miserably waiting for Shara to return from town with some type of magic cure that Tyler had guaranteed her would remove the smell—in a few days' time.

She no longer believed in magic, or even that she would someday return to normal. The only good thing that could be said for this moment was that her sense of smell seemed to have shut down completely, probably from overload, and she could no longer smell herself. She had tried walking around in hopes that exposure to the air would help. It hadn't. As she'd passed, she'd been sure she'd seen grass and weeds bending away from her to wither and die in the darkness. *She* wanted to wither and die, but instead, she'd sat down to wallow in misery.

Shara had left Bucky and Earl Junior with Erin and Tyler. The boys were perched together on the top fence of the corral. They were as far from their hosts as they could get and still legally be in the same county. Erin could barely make out their shining towheads in the darkness.

"Tell me something I don't know," she answered. The back porch light didn't reach very far across the yard.

"You stink real bad," Bucky emphasized as if she hadn't gotten the point the first time. His brother nodded vigorously.

Tyler chuckled, but when Erin gave him a murderous look, he disguised it as a cough. "I think she knows that, Bucky."

"I bet she didn't know skunks smelled so bad."

"She does now," Tyler answered.

"She from the city or somethin'?" Junior asked.

"Yeah. Tucson."

"Are people dumb in the city or somethin'?"

"Nah, they just don't have many skunks."

Erin's lips pinched together and she glared at the three males. Talk about being damned with faint praise. She thought of several responses, but none of them sounded any more intelligent than, "Oh, yeah?" so she kept her mouth shut.

Shara had been gone for half an hour and Tyler had assured Erin that she would return any minute. Erin wasn't sure that was such a good idea. Shara had been very direct in her questions about why Erin was at Tyler's house in the first place. Erin could understand the other woman's reaction. James Westin had told his female trainees to expect jealousy from their employers' women friends and acquaintances. Erin was hard-pressed to understand how Shara could be jealous of a woman who smelled as loathsome as she did.

Shara had expressed the opinion that Erin must be unbelievably stupid to have tangled with a skunk, a view she'd passed on to her sons before collecting some money from Tyler and heading into town in his truck. Erin didn't relish the idea of facing the woman again.

"Erin, what are you doing over there?" Tyler asked suddenly.

She glanced around morosely. "Killing the grass and all living creatures within a radius of five feet."

"There's a lawn chair," he said, pointing to an old-fashioned metal one on rocker legs.

"Oh, did you want the paint stripped off of it?"

This time he laughed out loud and Erin gave him another disgusted look. *Now* he cheers up, after being as sour as a lemon all day. There was reason for him to cheer up now, though. This time, she'd been on the receiving end of the disaster. The last shred of her professionalism had disappeared in this, the culmination of the day's fiascoes.

"You won't smell like this forever, Erin. It wears off eventually."

"Before or after I'm eligible for my old age pension?"

"I guess we'll have to wait and see."

"Oh, joy." She paused. "There is one good thing, though."

"What's that?"

"My sense of smell is completely gone. I can no longer smell myself."

"That's okay, lady," Bucky yelled. "We can smell you and you still stink real bad. You stink so bad, I wanna puke. I wanna puke and die."

"That's enough, Bucky," Tyler admonished him, but Erin still heard laughter in his voice.

Erin dropped her forehead to her knees once again, thinking sadly that she would never again sniff a flower or enjoy the aroma of baking muffins. How could she, when her olfactory nerves had been vaporized by 'Essence of Civet'?

She couldn't quite decide how everything had gone so wrong. The job had seemed so simple when Miss Eugenia had described it: take care of Tyler, care for his home, keep things running smoothly until he was better. Piece of cake, she'd thought. Piece of hell, it had turned out to be.

"I think we've settled one thing, Erin," Tyler said.

"Oh, what's that?"

"You'll have to stay. We can't let you go out in public. The health department would probably condemn you."

"Yeah," Junior added. "You'd get arrested."

"Locked up for a hundred years," Bucky added. "'Cause you smell real bad."

"I can't tell you how pleased I am to have my own little Greek chorus of doom," she answered. "Why don't you three take this act on the road?"

"Why, Miss Jones, I think your butler persona has cracked and shattered," Tyler said.

About half an hour ago, she wanted to point out, but she kept quiet. At that moment, Shara drove the truck into the yard, stopped and hopped out. She called for her boys to come help her and they scrambled to obey, the first time Erin had ever seen them do so. When Shara waved two candy bars, Erin understood why they'd been so prompt. No doubt, bribery was a way of life for them.

Shara jerked down the truck's tailgate and began pulling out case after case of something that rattled like glass. Erin stood to help, but when she saw what it was, she stared at Tyler. "Tomato juice?"

"Time honored cure. Didn't they teach you that in butler school?"

She answered through her teeth. "The subject never came up."

"Trust me, tomato juice works, but it takes a while."

She didn't believe that for a second, but she moved toward the truck anyway. Shara gave her a retiring look and she backed off, dropping her hands to her sides. It was probably best if she stayed down wind from Shara and her children, anyway. She didn't care for them much, but she didn't want their deaths on her conscience.

"I went to every store in town and I think this should be enough to do the trick. Someone at O'Hara's Market said the vet has some special shampoo you can use if this doesn't work, but it'd be pretty rough on your skin. You should try this first."

"Oh, I...why, thank you," Erin answered, surprised by Shara's thoughtfulness.

Tyler called for Junior to give his wheelchair a push. He rolled up beside the big galvanized washtub she'd dragged from the tack room at the back of the barn.

"Time for a bath, Miss Jones."

Her alarmed gaze shot from Tyler to Shara and her sons. "Bath?"

"That's what the tub's for, remember?"

"You need a bath, lady," Bucky jeered. "Nobody in the whole world stinks as bad as you!"

The adults ignored him. Tyler spoke to his brother. "Junior, pull it over by the back steps." The boy did so, with his little brother helping. Erin frowned, trying to understand what he had in mind.

When the truck was unloaded and the cases of tomato juice were stacked beside the tub, the boys jumped onto the tailgate, ripped open their candy bars and dug in.

Tyler said, "Thanks, Shara. I owe you one. We can take it from here."

The redhead squinted at him in the faint glow of the back porch light. "You want me to leave?"

"Yeah, and take the boys. We're going to have to soak in this stuff and we don't want an audience."

Erin turned and gaped at him. Surely she could have some privacy for this bath. "We?"

"The two of you together?" Shara squealed.

"I'll call for help if she tries to jump my bones," Tyler answered.

"Don't hold your breath," Erin snapped back.

Shara looked at Erin as though she were deciding whether she should stay and stake out her territory, but then her sons began pounding their boot heels against the sides of the truck, setting up a dreadful din.

"Tyler," Shara said, sharing a dubious look between Tyler and Erin. "This is a really bad idea. You ought to just run her off."

Erin's kind thoughts toward Shara disappeared.

"Where would she go?" Tyler asked.

"Back where she came from." Shara looked Erin up and down. "You don't need her here."

"I do for now," Tyler answered wearily.

It was obvious that Shara wanted to argue, but she

finally gathered her chocolate-smeared sons and headed home.

As the three of them disappeared down the lane, Tyler said, "Better strip, Erin, and get into the tub."

She turned on him. "Strip? What do you mean, strip?"

"I mean remove your clothes."

"Whatever for?"

"To get the skunk smell off your skin," he explained patiently.

Her mouth dropped open. "Are you kidding?"

"You don't intend to wear that damned suit, do you? What's the point since it has to be destroyed, anyway?"

"Destroyed?" she asked dully, looking down at it. It was the feminine version of the butler's "black and stripes," black jacket and dark gray striped trousers. Only today, as a concession to the June heat, she'd worn the matching skirt. She'd had it tailored especially for her so that it didn't bind under her arms as she worked and it fit her long-waisted figure perfectly.

With his good hand, he reached down and jerked open the top of one case. As he did so, he glanced up at her. "You've got to soak in this stuff and there's no point in wasting it on that uniform. It'll have to be burned."

Erin repressed a sigh. The suit reeked. He was right, of course. The smell would never come out.

"If you're afraid I'm going to see more than you want me to, you can turn off the porch light before you strip down to your Skivvies."

Her chin came up. "Fine. I'll do that."

Erin stalked up the stairs, jerked the screen door

open and reached in to flip off the light. She didn't know why she felt so insulted by his statement. He was right. She didn't want him to look at her, because she didn't want to see him laugh or sneer at her as he'd been doing all day. She was embarrassed, exhausted and sick. All she wanted to do was clean up as much as possible, and go to her room—wherever that may be. Her suitcase still sat in the living room where she'd abandoned it hours ago to talk to Miss Eugenia on the phone. It seemed that a lifetime's worth of catastrophes had happened since then.

By the time she rejoined Tyler, he had already opened a few bottles of the juice and was pouring them, one at a time, into the tub. She could barely see him in the gloom, but she could hear the liquid gurgling and splashing as it hit the tin. He seemed to be holding the bottles between his thighs and twisting off the lids with his uninjured hand. She didn't know how much of the juice she would need to soak in, or how long she'd need to soak. And she wasn't going to ask. She'd had enough conversation for one day. Battered by a confluence of sickness, anger and depression, Erin stood by the tub and kicked off her shoes.

Tyler squinted through the darkness. Only the barest sliver of moon gave light, but it was enough for him to see how reluctantly her hands lifted to take off her jacket. He'd begun to think it would have to be surgically removed. She started to fold it, but seemed to recall why she was removing it in the first place. With a shrug, she tossed it to the ground.

Next her hands went to the waistband of her skirt. Tyler had to admit he wasn't sorry to see it go, either.

It was ugly, formal, not at all what he would like to see her wear.

He shifted in his chair. That brought up the question of exactly what it was he would like to see her wear. He watched her fingers lift slowly to the buttons of her blouse. Actually the less the better was beginning to sound good to him. Hell, this day had been such a fiasco, he deserved to get some enjoyment from it.

He looked away. What kind of man had he become that he would sit ogling Doris Jones's daughter, the kid with the magenta hair and eyebrow ring, the girl who'd wanted to have the name Ricky tattooed on her butt?

He glanced back. This was no kid.

What he could see of her was womanly; lush and ripe. Her breasts swelled out of a low-cut bra that made his eyes widen. Who would have thought that prim and proper suit had hidden underwear like that? This was getting interesting. He wasn't even going to think about how weird it was for him to be having such thoughts about a woman who smelled as she did right now. He just kept his eyes wide and enjoyed the show.

Bending, she skimmed off a half slip and panty hose. Good, he thought. He hated panty hose, anyway. Stockings and garters were much more to his liking. He could see that her waist was tiny—he could span it with his hands—and her hips were just right. Not too full. Not too skinny.

He was disappointed to see that was as far as she intended to go in undressing. She expected to soak the smell away wearing her bra and panties. For a moment, he considered telling her she had to be completely naked in order for the tomato juice to work, but he figured she probably wouldn't fall for it—and she might grab one of these full bottles and take a swing at him for suggesting it.

"Get in," he said, and was surprised to hear that his voice was strained.

She glanced in his direction and he knew she was wondering what was wrong with his voice.

She did as he said, though, climbing carefully into the washtub and lowering herself until the thick liquid touched her bottom. A low sound of distress squeezed from her throat as it hit her skin.

"Think of it as medicine," he advised. "Here. I'll pour some of this on your back."

"Oh, goody."

Still fighting, he thought, with satisfaction. At least she wasn't crying. Not that he would have expected it of her. Tyler wondered at his own ambiguous feelings. One minute he wanted to strangle her, and the next he was admiring her courage.

Erin folded over in the tub and waited for him to pour the juice over her. Her pale skin gleamed with dull luminescence and he could see the arch of her narrow spine, the faint ridges of her shoulder blades. He swallowed hard, blessed the broken leg that kept him seated so he could avoid the embarrassment he would have experienced if he was able to stand and wondered again what kind of depraved individual he'd become to lust after a woman as distressed as she was. Obviously he'd been alone too long.

He'd already known that. As he'd told Erin, he didn't have any kind of a social life. Since he'd heard about this place from Earl Breslin, bought it and moved in, he'd done nothing but work. There was a bar up the highway where he could have gone any evening and been welcomed. There were women there. They would have welcomed him, too, but he wasn't interested. He'd seen too many of their type when he'd been on the rodeo circuit.

True, many of the girls who had followed the rodeo from stop to stop had only been looking for fun. He'd liked them. They'd hung around the entrance gate, greeting the contestants, wishing them luck, then meeting them later for drinks and dancing. Occasionally they'd gone off with the men, slept with them, but mostly they'd been girls with jobs and lives they had to get back to, so they'd left before it got too late and headed home.

There had been others, though, looking for something more disturbing—notches on their bedposts, the type of high they received from bragging to their friends about the cowboy they'd been with. He'd overheard such talk, been the subject of it, his prowess in bed discussed in terms that would make an old sailor blush.

Erin wasn't like that. Doris Jones was a lady and doubtless she'd raised her daughter to be a lady, too. The woman had taken a few wild turns in her life, but her basic decency had surfaced. He could see it in the tenseness of her body, the stiffness of her spine. She was humiliated by this. And he wasn't making it easy for her.

But worst of all, he lusted after her. And that, most certainly, was the biggest catastrophe of all.

5

It took a few minutes for Erin to accustom herself to the feel of the tomato juice on her skin. It was thick, rough-textured and cold. She steeled herself, prepared for Tyler to pour a bottle of the stuff on her back. Nothing happened.

She waited, not wanting to turn around to see what he was doing. She had passed major embarrassment long ago, but she didn't want to have to look at him, so she waited.

Still nothing. Finally she turned her head to see what he was doing. He had an opened bottle of juice in his hand, poised over her back. She couldn't see his eyes, but what she could see of his face was set and shuttered. After an hour of laughing at her, was he now angry?

"Tyler?" she asked hesitantly, her voice low. The stillness in his body made her stomach flutter, but this time it wasn't from nausea.

"Turn around," he said gruffly as he tilted the bottle and poured it over her back.

She jumped when it hit her skin and she whipped her head around. "It's cold."

"Sorry."

The gruffness in his voice made her turn around again, facing away from him. "How...how long is this going to take?" she asked after a moment.

"A hell of a lot longer than I'd like it to," he muttered.

"What?"

"Never mind. I don't know how long it will take. Soak for an hour and then we'll go into the house. You can have a real bath." He turned away to grab the bucket she'd brought him and began filling it with juice. He sat the bucket on his lap, turned slightly at the waist and plunged his arm in. He stuck his foot out, considered the toe of his boot and said, "This is the only limb I've got left that's not injured in some way. Care to give it a shot?"

Don't tempt me, Erin thought, but she pinched her lips together and said nothing. So, they were back to sarcasm and irritation. All right. She could deal with that because it didn't give her the kind of strange, quaking flutters that she'd felt when he had looked at her a few minutes ago.

As Tyler had prescribed, they soaked for an hour—a silent hour. To her relief, Erin noticed that the smell did seem to dissipate somewhat—either that, or her sense of smell truly was dead.

When their time was up, Erin stood, dripping tomato juice, and cursed herself for forgetting to find some towels. She should have thought of it. She would have thought of it if she hadn't been so unnerved. Hurriedly she stepped from the tub and scurried up the porch steps, grabbed some rags from a box by the door and was glad to see that one of them was an old shirt of Tyler's. Gratefully she pulled it on, buttoned the few remaining buttons securely, then went back outside to help him up the steps and onto the porch. The day's shocks and exertions were beginning to catch up to her. She swayed on her feet, gazed at him from beneath eyelids drooping with exhaustion and said, "Where's my room, Tyler?"

"For tonight, right here," he answered.

"On the porch?"

"We'll both sleep here tonight, or we'll never get the skunk smell out of the house."

"Oh" was all she could think of to say. Of course, he was right, but she'd been desperate to get into a room of her own and close the door. Have some privacy. Burst into tears.

It wasn't to be. Banking her disappointment, she pushed him into the house, to his room and to the doorway of the bathroom beyond. "I can take it from here," he said gruffly. "Come back after your shower and we'll figure out what we're going to do about beds out there."

Nodding, she turned away, retrieved her suitcase from the living room and did as he said, showering in the bathroom off the hallway. The smell seemed a little better afterward, there didn't seem to be any in her hair, which she washed and combed out, long and wavy over her shoulders. Seeing it, hope buoyed inside her. Maybe she would return to normal, after all. When she was dressed in her pale blue nightgown and had the matching robe buttoned up to her chin, she returned to get Tyler.

He had cleaned up, too. Though his eyes were rimmed with bruised exhaustion, he looked better. It didn't help to know that she was responsible for most of that exhaustion.

"Are you ready?" she asked, hesitating in the doorway.

He looked up, his gaze skimming over her. His

dark eyes narrowed and his mouth took on a cynical slant. "Back to being Miss Prim and Proper, I see."

Erin ignored that. She didn't care what he said now. Slowly, but surely, she was regaining control of herself and she wasn't going to let go again as she had before. Snapping and verbal sparring weren't the way to survive this assignment.

"Are you ready?" she repeated, though she could see that he was. The tomato juice was gone from his arm, and chest, and he'd washed up. Water dampened his dark hair, which he'd finger-combed out of his face. She couldn't imagine how he'd done that with only one good hand, but she wasn't foolish enough to ask.

Tyler told her where to find some old blankets and sheets, which had probably been in the house when he'd bought it. She found a couple of decrepit camp cots that had to be placed side by side on the crowded porch. She held the chair while Tyler maneuvered out of it and onto his bed, stretching out full-length. When she bent to place a pillow under his cast, he reached up and grabbed her wrist.

With a startled squeak, she glanced up.

"Don't start that again," he growled. "It was hard enough to take when you smelled like a woman."

Furious, she slapped the pillow down beside the cot, flipped off the porch light and lay down on the narrow bed beside his.

Silence stretched between them, punctuated by the sound of crickets in the backyard. The wind kicked up, sending a welcome, fresh breeze drifting over them.

"Well, Delightful Jones, this has been a hell of a day," Tyler said in the darkness.

Erin, lying as stiff as a freshly sawn board answered, "Yes, it has. And it's been a pleasure to serve you, sir."

He chuckled, but it sounded rusty. "Go to sleep, Erin, so we can get up in the morning and see what other delights you've got in store."

"You can't even imagine," she said tightly.

"Yes, I can. That's the trouble."

"TIME TO RISE AND SHINE, tenderfoot."

Erin heard the command, but she responded by groaning miserably, scooting lower in the nest of covers and pulling the sheet over her head. She was exhausted from bad dreams involving foul-smelling animals, which if her fuzzy memories were at all reliable, seemed to be skunks having wheelchair races.

"No dice. Come on now, wake up."

The sheet was tugged away from her face and sunlight scored a direct hit in her eyes. She squawked and threw her arm over her face. Forcing her out of bed was one of her brother Mark's favorite morning pastimes.

"Come on, Jonesy, get up." Her shoulder received a nudge, none-too-gently.

"Darn it, Mark, knock it off," she grumbled.

"Who the hell is Mark?"

At the gruff question, memory and recognition flooded Erin's brain. Her eyes flew open, her arm sprang away from her face, and her head jerked toward the voice.

Tyler Morris sat on the bunk beside her. His dark hair was tumbled over his forehead, his eyes were sleepy. He'd removed his shirt and tossed it on the floor beside his cot. Erin was fascinated to see that he was as lean and muscular as she had suspected. The soft hair on his chest formed a T, running from nipple to nipple, then scooping inward, rippling over washboard abdominal muscles and disappearing in the unbuttoned waistband of his cutoff jeans.

Erin swallowed hard. This was not the kind of early-morning sight that should greet a woman who wanted to keep her wits intact. Not that she necessarily wanted to at that moment. She wondered if that hair was as soft as it looked and if it continued narrowing down to...

Heavens! Erin's eyes shot up to meet Tyler's. He was watching her with a knowing expression.

"Good morning," he said.

"Goo...hoo...hood morning." To her dismay, she could feel a blush climbing her throat and landing in her face where it lingered as if it had been painted on. Self-consciously, she touched her cheek, feeling the heat there, then shoved the long, curly tangle of hair back from her temple.

"Well?" he asked, his voice low and morning-rough.

"Huh?" Her mouth couldn't seem to work any quicker than her brain.

"Who's Mark? Your boyfriend?"

"My brother," she answered, wondering at the hard note in his voice. "He used to like to drag me out of bed in the mornings. He said he was trying to keep me from being late for school." She didn't know why she'd added that last bit. It wasn't relevant.

"Were you late?" Tyler asked, leaning forward and propping his elbow on his knee. His gaze swept her once again and she was glad for the sheet and blanket that covered her.

"All the time," she sighed.

"What would they say about that at butler school?"

"They wouldn't care. I outgrew it."

"Bully for you. In that case, you won't mind rolling out of bed early to get started on the work around here."

Erin blinked. "Does that mean you're really letting me stay?"

He'd said so last night, but she needed confirmation.

"Smelling like you do, how could I let you loose in public?"

"Thank you so much," she said in a snippy tone, then bit her lip. She had to regain her professionalism if she intended to stay.

His lips twitched reluctantly. "Besides, who else would want you, except maybe a skunk of the opposite sex?"

Erin gave him a superior look that told him it was in very bad taste to mention the obvious. They still smelled awful—her especially—but it wasn't as nauseating as it had been the night before. Still, she knew it wasn't going to get any better for a few days so she would have to stay. Her first reaction was dismay, but then she realized it would suit her purpose. She could stay and pay off her debts.

"Then it looks as if I'd better get to work," she said in an expectant tone. She waited, hoping he would turn away so she could search for her robe, which she suspected had been kicked to the floor. He

Patricia Knoll   81

gave her a glance that told her he knew what she wanted, but for a minute he didn't move.

"If you're going to stay, we've got to talk about what your job's going to include," he said with a frown.

She curled her fingers around the top of the sheet. "That sounds sensible."

Erin held the sheet up to her chin and eased over to scan the floor. Nothing. Darn it, why didn't Tyler leave so she could search properly?

"I'm the boss," he went on. "So don't get any ideas about trying to take over and run the place like Eugenia would."

Erin squirmed her way to the other side of the cot, but she couldn't get far because Tyler blocked her way. She gave him a frustrated look, but she kept her tone matter-of-fact. "I have no plans to take over. I'm just the butler."

"Fine, because there can only be one boss," he said sternly. "If this was a marriage I would definitely be wearing the pants in the family." He said this with a nod, then turned and stuck his feet out as he prepared to move off her cot.

Marriage? Erin wondered where that came from. In fact, where was all this pontificating coming from? She glanced down and spied her robe. "I understand that you want to wear the pants, but in the meantime, could I have my robe back?"

He glanced down. Her pale blue robe was wrapped around his cast, the lacy collar delicate against the thick plaster. He harrumphed, gave her a look that dared her to laugh, and whipped it off his leg. He tossed it to her, then scooted down the length of her cot, grabbed the wheelchair and maneuvered himself into it. While he was doing that, Erin hustled into her robe, fighting a grin as she did so. Seeing him looking silly had cheered her up.

When Erin was on her feet, she reached for the handles of the wheelchair, but Tyler growled, "Don't start that again. I can take care of this chair. I intend to be out of it in a day or so and back on the crutches."

Erin didn't doubt for a second that he would. She could see that he still favored his sprained wrist, gingerly grasping the outer rim of the wheel to direct it where he wanted to go. Watching him use his wrist without wincing, she marveled at his remarkable powers of recuperation.

Staring with fascination, she observed as he backed out of the area by the cots, turned and rolled into the house. She already knew he was a man of unusual determination and everything he did seemed to prove that further.

Erin gathered her things, showered yet again—in hopes of removing more of the skunk's scent—and dressed quickly in the gray slacks that went with her ruined uniform, and a white shirt. Even though this job wasn't turning out to be anything she'd been trained for, she wanted to maintain the standards she'd been taught.

Tyler didn't agree. When they met in the kitchen half an hour later, he frowned at her from the neat bun on top of her head to her flat-heeled black shoes. Her pumps had been ruined along with her uniform.

"Don't you own any jeans?" Tyler asked.

"Sure." She'd brought one pair and some shorts for her days off—if she had any.

"Look," he said. "This is the way it goes around

here. You've got to dress for the job.'' He gave her another critical look. ''The hair's all right,'' he said after a moment. ''It'll stay out of your way. You need a short-sleeved shirt, those pants have got to go. Put on your jeans. What about boots? Got any?''

''Uh, no,'' she admitted. She didn't like his criticism, but he knew what kind of work she was going to be doing and how she should dress for it.

''Sneakers?''

''Yes. I'll put them on.'' She turned away. Tyler hadn't assigned a bedroom to her, so she'd chosen one for herself. It was the farthest one from his, had a double bed with a depressingly faded brown bedspread, and a scarred chest of drawers. She changed clothes, hurrying because it was her job to cook breakfast, but when she returned to the kitchen wearing her jeans and a white T-shirt, she saw that Tyler had poured himself a bowl of cereal. She gave him a disappointed look. ''If I'm going to stay, you have to let me do my job.''

He put his spoon down. ''Listen, you're not going to make me toast cut into perfect triangles with the crusts sliced off. You're not going to cook my eggs to perfection. You're not going to warm my newspaper by the fireplace to set the ink so it doesn't come off on my hands. I don't even take the newspaper because I don't have time to read it.''

Erin opened her mouth, then shut it, surprised by his vehemence. ''Yes, sir.''

That really infuriated him. ''And call me Tyler, damn it! Forget the 'sir' stuff. Around here, you're not a butler. You're a ranch hand.''

This time his tone snapped a reaction out of her. Before she stopped to think, she whipped her hand up to her forehead to deliver a smart salute. "Yes, sir!"

She froze, and Tyler grinned. "I said forget the 'sir' stuff," he reminded her.

Her lips tightened and she moved across the kitchen to prepare her own breakfast. Just to show him she wasn't giving in completely, she made coffee, poured him a mug of it and served it on the same tray she'd used the night before.

Tyler watched her, still grinning. He liked her better this way, sparring with him. It kept things less personal and more interesting. And since she'd arrived, things had been far from dull.

He didn't know exactly when he'd made the decision to let her stay. Last night he'd gone to sleep thinking he would run her off in the morning. Skunk-bombed or not, he'd been determined to make her pack her bags, head out and leave him alone.

He'd awakened with his leg throbbing, looked over at her tangled golden hair peeking from beneath the sheet, her slim form snuggled into the lumpy cot and decided he'd let her stick around.

It was a mistake.

He knew that. He'd convinced himself of that last night. He'd thought about it carefully, given himself every possible reason to send her away—the fact that there was no way he could think of her as anything other than a desirable woman being first on his list.

Something about this situation reminded him of when he'd left his parents' house. It had been twelve years ago. They'd expected him to go to college, get a business degree and take over the family business eventually. He couldn't do it.

He'd wanted to be a cowboy. There'd been no

logic to it. He could ride but he knew little about the life of a rodeo cowboy. Against all logic, he'd gone after it. He'd never regretted his decision, though he knew it had been hard on his parents.

He was doing it again. Against all logic, he was going to let Erin stay. Almost certainly he would regret his decision this time, but it had been so long since he'd been around any woman besides Shara, it might be worth it to take the risk. Of course, if he hurt her, his aunt Eugenia would kill him. He sat back, sipped his coffee and watched Erin as she moved around the kitchen.

Damn, she looked good in those jeans. Maybe it wasn't a mistake to keep her around, after all. She sure improved the scenery.

"Are you ready?" he asked when she'd finished cleaning up the kitchen.

"Certainly," she answered, her green eyes cool.

He knew she was mad at him. She wasn't going to forgive him for a while, but at least she wouldn't quit on him. She would attempt any job he gave her just to prove she could do it. There was a lot to be said for stubbornness. He was a master of it.

When the phone rang, she answered it in a crisp manner that set his teeth on edge. She was at it again.

"Morris residence. Certainly. May I ask who's calling?" She paused and shot Tyler a startled glance, but she recovered quickly. "Yes, Mr. Wettig—Sam— No, you weren't interrupting anything."

Tyler couldn't hold back a chuckle when she handed the phone to him. He wasn't sure what had set Sam off on his romantic notions, but he'd been trying to marry off himself and all of his friends for months now. It seemed that Erin didn't find it amusing.

He took the phone from her. "Yes, Sam?"

"Ty, I took another look up on the mesa again at daylight this morning and all along Diamond Creek. I thought that bunch you drove up there would be bedded down somewhere, but I couldn't find a sign of them. Want me to keep trying?"

"Nah, you've got your own work to do," Tyler said, irritated and mystified by his wandering herd. He didn't know what had happened to them. Twenty head didn't just disappear without help. They weren't smart enough for that. "I'll go myself," he said, thanking Sam and hanging up.

He looked at Erin. "Can you drive my pickup?"

She glanced out the window dubiously. The hulking black vehicle sat where Shara had parked it the night before to unload the tomato juice. "Well..." she began.

"Shara can," he added, knowing it was a dirty trick. "If you can't handle it, I can ask her." Shara had grown up on a ranch and driven farm equipment since she was twelve.

"Of course I can," Erin said smartly.

"Then let's go. You're going to drive me up to the mesa to look for those cattle."

Her face seemed to pale. "You can get there by truck?"

"Yeah, but it's rough. Horse is better." He reached down and tapped his cast. "But, obviously, I can't do that."

"All right," she said, lifting her chin. "Just tell me where to drive."

Tyler nodded, wondering why she suddenly

looked as if she was ready to face a firing squad. "I will. Before we go, we've got to take care of the stock."

She gave him a careful look. "I take it you mean the horses?"

Tyler felt a grin pulling at his lips. Last night, she'd looked ready to bolt when she'd been around the animals. She didn't act as if she wanted to do it again, but she was here for the duration.

"Just turn them out in the pasture," he said, watching relief bloom in her eyes. "You'll have to doctor one of the heifers later. Sam tells me she's got a cut on the right side of her rump...must have scraped a branch." This time he saw her initial nervous reaction washed away by sympathy.

She lifted her chin. "I can do it."

Damned if she couldn't, he thought.

HE WAS TESTING HER. She knew it and she was determined to prove herself. He expected her to cave in, to quit, but she wouldn't.

While he watched, Erin strode briskly out to the barn, swung the door open and went through to let the animals out of their stalls and into the pasture. True, she swung each stall door open and scrambled onto the nearest railing when the horse passed, but Tyler couldn't see her, so she didn't care. It gave her a vantage point where she could watch the beautiful horses step past on their long, graceful legs, the two babies frisking beside their mothers.

In spite of her initial apprehension, and their fear of her offensive smell, Erin was enchanted. She would enjoy learning more about them, maybe even learn to ride one. Tyler couldn't show her. She wouldn't have asked him, anyway, but maybe she could teach herself.

She closed the door that lead to the pasture and glanced around at the saddles and other gear that hung on the walls. Everything was within easy reach, but she thought it could be better organized. She would give it some thought. In the meantime, Tyler was waiting for her. With a sense of dread, she left the barn and walked to where he waited at the bottom of the steps.

Immediately he pointed to the behemoth of a truck. "The keys are in it. Let's go." Then he paused. "Have you got a swimsuit with you?"

"No." She blinked at him. "Why would I need one?" she asked suspiciously.

He sighed. "Try to help the girl and all I get is grief." He jerked his chin upward. "Go get a change of clothes."

"What?"

"And a couple of towels."

"Whatever for?"

"You may need them. Go ahead."

She opened her mouth, ready to argue.

He said, "Aren't you supposed to do what I say?"

"Within reason," she muttered, turning and trudging toward her bedroom. She returned with a pair of shorts and a tank top.

He looked them over. "I approve. The butler's wardrobe is becoming more to my liking as the day progresses."

"I'm so glad," she answered demurely and he gave a dry laugh, but he didn't explain why she would need them.

Erin turned to the truck and wondered with a sink-ing heart what she had gotten herself into. Darn it, why was she so stubborn? Why couldn't she admit to Tyler that she'd never driven such a big vehicle before? That if it had a stick shift, she could be in serious trouble? It had been many years since she'd driven a stick shift and that had been in her brother Dave's little red English sports car.

Because he'd thrown Shara's name into it and Erin had been foolish enough to feel a spike of jealousy, which had made her mad at herself and fueled her determination even more.

Erin pushed Tyler's chair close to the side of the truck. He swung himself inside while she returned the wheelchair to the bottom of the back steps. She could have left it where it was, beside the truck, but she dawdled, dreading the moment when she had to get into the truck and pretend that she knew what she was doing. James Westin had definitely never covered the operation of ranch vehicles in his courses. Why couldn't Tyler have asked her to go into town and buy him a box of cigars? Or make an appointment with his tailor? Or chill a bottle of Chablis by wrapping it in dampened newspaper and holding it out the window of a speeding car? Those things she could do!

When Tyler turned to give her a curious look from beneath his thick, black brows, Erin knew she had to quit stalling. Trying to look as efficient as possible, she strode to the truck, climbed inside and slammed the door. Immediately the smell they'd both been ignoring punched the air. They dove for the window cranks, wound the glass down and took grateful gulps of the fresh air that flowed in.

Once her head cleared, Erin reached for the key,

pumped the gas pedal with a couple of quick taps of her sneakered foot and ground the ignition. She was gratified when the engine sprang to life.

Displaying a confidence she didn't feel, she placed her foot on the clutch, pushed it to the floor, moved the floor-mounted gearshift out of neutral and into first gear, then pressed on the gas.

And promptly crushed Tyler's wheelchair up against the porch steps.

"Hey!" Tyler shouted when metal shrieked against metal. He bounced on the seat, grabbed for the dashboard when Erin hit the brakes and whipped his head around to look out the window. "What the hell are you doing?" He waved his arms at her. "Put it in first! Put it in first!"

"You don't have to yell," she insisted. "I'm sitting right next to you. I can hear just fine."

"Did you just hear the sound of a wheelchair being destroyed?" he demanded.

She had no answer to that. Of course, she'd heard it.

"Put this thing in first gear," he said, in a tight voice. "And move forward."

"It is in..." Her voice trailed off as she looked down at the gearshift lever. It clearly showed she was in reverse. She stared at it. "I don't know how that happened."

"The truck didn't do it on its own," he said wearily.

She pinched her lips together and lifted her chin. Crying would be totally inappropriate. "No, it's my fault," she said, hating the breathy catch in her voice.

"You've at least got that right. Go forward," he repeated, his voice harried. He threw his hands in the direction he wanted her to go. She did so, wrestling the gearshift into the right place and pulling forward until he shouted, "Stop."

With her foot on the brake, she twisted around to look at the wheelchair. Heads together, she and Tyler stared at the damage. The left wheel of the chair was bent and twisted, making the chair lean drunkenly to the side. As they watched, it swayed, then clattered to the ground, its one good wheel spinning slowly in the air. "I know just how you feel, fella," Tyler said sympathetically to the broken chair.

She gave him a disgruntled look. He didn't have to rub it in.

"It was a loaner from the hospital," he went on.

"I wonder how much it cost."

"I don't know, but you'll find out when you get the bill," he said, turning to look at her. His dark eyes regarded her with a kind of horrified awe. "Have you always been a one-woman demolition crew?"

"Certainly not," she snapped. "This is a... temporary problem." A very recent temporary problem.

Tyler lifted an eyebrow at her. "It only started yesterday when you walked into my life," he said, echoing her thoughts. "Lucky me." With a gusty sigh, he sat back, carefully arranged his leg so the cast wouldn't pinch and said in a fatalistic tone, "Drive on, Jonesy. It's only eight o'clock in the morning, who knows what else you can accomplish before nightfall?"

"That's completely unfair," she said, double-checking to make sure she was in the right gear. She was extremely careful as she drove out of the yard and past the little house across the way. Shara came out onto the porch and watched them creep past. "I just had a little accident," Erin pointed out to Tyler. When the engine began to whine, she shifted into second gear. It took a couple of tries before she ground it into the correct gear. Beside her, Tyler's face held the look of a man having his teeth extracted without anesthesia. "And it was only because I'm not accustomed to driving such a big truck," she went on defensively. Or any truck, she thought, but she didn't say it out loud. "Why do you have such a big truck, anyway?" she asked recklessly, still stung and embarrassed about ramming the wheelchair. She shifted into third gear more successfully.

"Ranch work?" he suggested. "This is a working ranch, you know, though with you around, it may not be working much longer."

She pinched her lips together and didn't answer. There was no point in prolonging the argument. He was right, though she wouldn't admit it. She had never been seriously accident-prone before. She didn't understand what was wrong with her since she'd been around him. Nothing seemed to go right. If this series of disasters got out, her career could be in tatters.

For some reason, she recalled an old movie with Gary Cooper called *Casanova Brown*. In it, he'd been responsible for one disaster after another until he'd succeeded in burning down the home of his bride's family. Erin fervently hoped things got better for her before they reached that stage.

6

WHEN SHE DIDN'T RESPOND to his taunt, Tyler sighed and told her which direction to take. She followed the highway to a dirt track that wound through mesquite bushes and ocotillo cactus. It was slow going, but she managed well once she became accustomed to driving the big truck with its high wheels.

"I bought it when I was going on down the road," he said suddenly.

She slowed to negotiate a narrow wash, then gave him a puzzled look once they were on the other side. "Well, all trucks go down the road. I mean, isn't that what they're supposed to do?"

He shook his head. "No, tenderfoot, that's not what I mean. Going on down the road is what people call it when they follow the rodeo circuit, entering the events, trying to win money."

"Oh."

Tyler leaned back, rested his arm on the open window and looked out across the desert. "It's a way of life, and this truck pulled a trailer with all my things in it so I could go where I wanted to, earn the money I needed."

Erin gave him a quick, sideways glance, amazed that he was opening up to her this way. They'd known each other less than twenty-four hours and theirs certainly wasn't the kind of relationship where confidences would be shared like this. She was secretly thrilled. "So you could buy your place," she said. When he looked at her, she added with a little shrug, "Miss Eugenia told me."

"Yeah. I wanted my own place. I didn't want to be indebted...." He paused. "Not to anyone."

That's why he hadn't asked his wealthy aunt for money. Erin knew nothing about his parents, but they might be well-off, too. He hadn't taken their help, either.

"I like being on my own, being independent. Free."

"Most people do," Erin responded, though she didn't know quite where this conversation was leading. Was he warning her away from a romantic interest in him? He was wasting his breath, she thought self-righteously. She had none.

From the corner of her eye, she glanced at his long, lean body, his muscled arms dusted with silky dark hair, his big, strong hands, one resting on the window frame, the other on the seat beside them.

No romantic interest at all.

"These missing cattle are part of my freedom," he went on. "They're my livelihood. That's why I've got to go see if I can find them."

That made sense, and in spite of her irritation with him, she admired his determination to be self-reliant.

Tyler directed her to drive up a narrow wash that topped out on the mesa. She took it at a crawl, and in first gear, but they made it and she felt a tremendous surge of accomplishment. Strangely having negotiated the wash without getting the truck hung up on a rock gave her the same satisfaction she'd experienced when she'd successfully arranged for the single remaining seat on the Concorde for Lord Vincent.

At last, she felt as if she'd done something right.

Once they reached the top of the mesa, they inched along, with Tyler awkwardly leaning his head out the window. He watched the ground for hoof marks or tracks of any kind.

"Nothing," he said, sitting back and shaking his head. "It's like they've been picked up and swept away by a spaceship."

"How many did you say were here?" she asked, her gaze darting from the track to his worried face.

"Thirty," he said. "Some heifers with their calves and a couple of yearlings. I hadn't even branded the calves yet, and I planned to sell the yearlings at auction next month." He pointed to a stand of cottonwoods that flanked a creek cutting through the mesa. A few cows stood in the shade. "Those are the ones Sam found."

Though she didn't know much about ranching, she could interpret what he said about the missing cattle. Unbranded calves meant he couldn't identify them as his and yearlings, which she thought must mean year-old cattle, had been fattened on his land, but would now be sold for profit by whoever had stolen them. The yearlings would be branded, of course, but that wouldn't matter once they were killed and butchered.

Tyler had her slowly circle the mesa again while he leaned out, searching. He muttered under his breath about the restrictions of his broken leg. "I could cover a hell of a lot more ground on horseback."

Erin didn't answer. She was struck suddenly by

the unfairness of it, the downright criminality of stealing from a man who was already having troubles. The angry set of his jaw told her he didn't see himself as a victim, though. He was more the avenger type.

After they had finished their circuit of the mesa, Tyler sat back with a disgusted grunt. "Too much wind up here. If there were any tracks, they've blown away." He pointed to the right. "Turn down here."

They had reached an area that had a downward track that resembled an actual road.

"What is it?" This wasn't too bad, she thought with pleasure as she took the trail he indicated. It was wide enough for her to see where she was going.

"It's a mineral hot spring. The only one on my land."

"You mean, like a natural spa?"

"Yeah, only the water's thick with salts so it's undrinkable. It smells bad, but..."

"It probably smells better than skunk," she added, looking at him with delight in her green eyes. "You're a pal, Tyler." Especially after all the disasters she'd brought on him, she thought.

"Don't tell anyone. I'm trying to keep up my image of being a combination of a hanging judge, an outlaw and an ax murderer, mostly to keep Junior and Bucky in line. They only respect force."

"I'll remember that," she said. She reached a small valley and drove a few hundred feet to a tiny pool fed by a hot spring. The area immediately surrounding the water was free of vegetation, telling her that it was, indeed, full of salts and other naturally occurring chemicals that weren't good for plants. She stopped the truck and Tyler pointed to an outcropping of rocks nearby.

"Your changing room," he said.

Eagerly Erin stepped from the truck, grabbed her shorts, tank top and towel, and headed for the rocks. The tomato juice and two showers hadn't fully erased the odor. She had resigned herself to smelling like something no cat would bother to drag in, but she was willing to try a mineral bath. Even a mud bath, if necessary. It couldn't possibly be any worse.

The rocks made an effective screen as she changed, but she wished she'd brought a change of underwear, too. She would have to wear the shorts and top with nothing underneath. The fabric wasn't particularly thin, but that wouldn't matter once it was wet. It couldn't be helped, though, and if there was a chance that she could get rid of this smell, or at least receive some relief from it, she was willing to try anything. Besides, what could be worse than the embarrassment she'd already suffered? She stepped out from behind the rocks with more boldness than she felt.

Tyler had made his way from the truck, spread a towel on the gravel that edged the pool, lain down full-length on it and plunged his arm in. She felt sorry for him. The position couldn't be comfortable for his leg, but he was probably as desperate as she was, especially since he couldn't take a real bath until the cast came off.

Carrying her own towel, Erin walked to the pool, stepping carefully over the sharp rocks. She winced as they dug into the soles of her feet, thinking that she was exactly what Tyler had called her first thing that morning. A tenderfoot.

Tyler watched her as she stepped gingerly into the pool, but she didn't meet his eyes. The water was warm, too warm for this June morning, but it felt good. Erin reached out a hand to steady herself, moving with great care because she couldn't see her feet in the murky water.

"There's a ledge over here," Tyler said. "You can sit down."

She followed his instructions, moving to the ledge near him and sitting down. She immediately slipped sideways.

"I should have told you. The minerals make the water especially buoyant. It's hard to sit down and stay in one place."

"No kidding." Erin tried to keep her bottom on the ledge, but she slithered around as if she'd been greased. She finally found a handhold on each side of the ledge and settled down, only to discover to her amazement that the water made her breasts more buoyant, too. They floated up as if they each had their own little life jacket attached. Quickly she submerged up to her neck.

Miraculously she discovered that the skunk scent was hardly noticeable, masked by the water's own odor, which was metallic and slightly sulfuric. She could only hope the effect would continue after she climbed out and dried off. She would much rather smell like a rusty bucket than a skunk.

"I think it's helping," she said, turning her head and discovering that she had floated closer to him than she'd thought.

"Yeah," Tyler answered, his eyes on her face. "We may have found a better treatment than tomato juice."

"Yes," she said. Her voice was faint, but she knew it wasn't in reaction to the hot water. It was in reaction to Tyler Morris. He was close and in spite of his injuries, vital, compelling and focused on her.

She took a breath, but it didn't cool her off. She knew her naturally curly hair was beginning to kink around her face in tiny corkscrews, her face was flushed from the heat.

"We're, uh, going to smell like people again," she said inanely.

"Yeah," he said again. He leaned closer, his gaze going from her lips to her eyes, then back again.

He was going to kiss her.

HE WAS GOING TO KISS HER.

Tyler didn't even think about the impulse, he only went with it. His leg throbbed, his wrist ached, gravel and rocks dug into his stomach, but he didn't give them a thought. When Erin lifted her head, he leaned in and hitched himself a little closer.

This was the kind of moment he hadn't experienced in years. He felt exactly as he had when he'd lowered himself to the bare back of a bronc, wrapped the rope around his right hand and put his left hand in the air. The anticipation was the same as when he had given the nod to the crew to open the chute allowing the bronc to explode into the ring where he would try his best to buck Tyler off his back—and maybe break the man's neck.

Tyler knew this, felt the surge of anticipation and touched his lips to hers.

She could have moved away. She could have splashed the salty water in his face. That would have stopped him cold, but she didn't budge. Instead those curious green eyes of hers watched him, asking what he was going to do and why he was going to do it.

Damned if he knew.

When he brushed her lips, he discovered they were as soft as he'd suspected they would be. He turned his head and tested the skin of her cheek. Soft there, too. He came back to her mouth, pressed his lips to hers and lingered. There was a moment of resistance in her, a brief stiffness in her jaw, but he didn't let her have time to allow it to grow. He brought his arm around so that she was held firmly against the slick rocks, exactly where he wanted her.

His lips found hers, pressing firmly, molding her softness to his. She tasted sweet, womanly—delightful, in fact. She didn't respond, but at this moment, he didn't care. Right now, this was for him. He thought about waking yesterday and finding her staring at him, awareness in her eyes. He thought about seeing her body, slim and graceful, as she'd lowered herself into the washtub. Those had fed his eyes. Now he fed his taste.

He wanted more so he took it, giving the barest thought to recalling that only the night before, he hadn't wanted this at all. His fingers slid beneath the straps of her tank top to trace the bones of her shoulders, to skim over the velvet of her skin. He slipped the strap down, then tore his lips from hers to bury them in the bend of her neck.

Shivers trembled through her. He could hear her breath catch in her throat. He took that as a promising sign, until she said, "Tyler, don't. Don't do this."

He could feel the tremble in her hands as they floated upward to push him away.

Reluctantly he lifted his head and looked into eyes that were troubled, edged with worry and surprise.

"Why did you do that?" she asked, her breathy voice marked by accusation.

"Impulse," he said, and watched as the doubt in her eyes was swept away by cool fury.

"You're not an impulsive man," she said in a frosty tone. She moved away, slipped, righted herself and bobbed in the shallow pool.

"Sure I am." He knew he was lying. "Why did you let me kiss you?"

He could see she had no answer to that. At least, not one she would say to him. Her jaw trembled, making him feel like the jerk he was.

He looked around at the spring that bubbled up out of the ground and fed the pool. He still didn't know why he had brought her here, though it wasn't for the reason she thought. He couldn't convince her of that, though. His only excuse was that in the past twenty-four hours he seemed to be doing many things he didn't want to do. The one thing he did want to do, which was to make love to her, was beyond him as long as he had this cast on his leg— and as long as he had a speck of decency in him.

HE HAD KISSED HER. And she had let him, hadn't even given a token resistance until it had been too late. Why hadn't she thought? It had been years, well, at least months, since she'd done anything without considering the consequences. She thought she'd outgrown such stupidity.

Distressed, Erin turned her back on Tyler, moved across the pool and leaned out, reaching for her towel. When her fingers closed around it, she climbed out without a backward glance, whipped it around her and scurried to the rock outcropping where she'd left her clothes. She could tell that the skunk smell had all but disappeared and she almost wept with gratitude. At least one good thing had come from this episode.

"Stupid, stupid," she muttered as she peeled off her wet things.

Getting involved with Tyler by even so much as a kiss was an abysmally stupid thing to do. It was as unprofessional as she could get. Even if she hadn't already known that, it was something James Westin had drilled into the heads of his butler trainees— especially the women. The confines of a home, of shared responsibilities, created unusual intimacies that could lead to romantic entanglements. These always ended badly, resulting in the butler getting fired. She knew all these things, and yet she'd let Tyler kiss her, anyway.

Her movements were jerky and distraught as she dried herself off, and climbed back into her jeans and T-shirt in record time.

She was angry with Tyler, angrier with herself, wanted to streak back to the house, jump in her car and put miles between them, and yet she couldn't. She was committed to stay.

Why had he kissed her? It had ruined everything, changed the nature of their relationship beyond repair—unless she could ignore it.

Erin paused as she was tying her shoe. That was it. She would ignore it. She would pull her professionalism around her as if it were a cloak, stick strictly to her job and not allow any more such— aberrations to occur between them. Tyler didn't like her uniforms, he didn't like her job, he didn't like having her around and he certainly wouldn't like this, but he would have to live with it. That decided, she finished dressing, smoothed the dismay from her face, grabbed her wet things and marched from behind the rocks carrying her wet things.

Tyler was already inside the truck and he gave her a wary look when her shorts and tank top landed in the truck bed with a splat. "Thank you for bringing me here, Tyler," she said in a voice cool enough to make a polar bear feel right at home. "It really helped get rid of the smell."

"You're welcome," he said cautiously. He waited as if he expected her to say something more about the kiss, but she started the truck, asked directions back to the house and drove there in silence.

When they returned to the house, Erin was anxious to scurry off to her room, or find a job she could do alone, but Tyler had other ideas.

"We've got to doctor that heifer," he said. "And I'm using 'we' in the loosest possible way. You'll have to do it, but park the truck by the pen and I'll tell you what to do."

Happy to concentrate on any kind of work, Erin obeyed. When she reached the pen, she saw the heifer waiting patiently by the water trough. When he drove her in, Sam had thrown down some hay for her and she continued to eat her way through it, placidly munching away while Erin followed Tyler's instructions to fetch a bottle of disinfectant from the barn, along with some big cotton swabs.

The cow ignored Erin as she sidled up. She didn't want Tyler to think she was afraid of this cow, but she couldn't help comparing the animal's size to her own. She looked at the hooves. If Miss Heifer decided to step on her foot, Erin knew it would break. It still ached from being closed in Tyler's front door yesterday.

In a gentle voice, she cooed, "Nice cow," as she approached.

Tyler snorted. "She's not a baby, Erin, and she's not wild. Walk right up behind her and doctor that cut, but watch her hooves."

"Don't worry. I intend to." Erin dipped the swab in the disinfectant and held it before her as if it were a sword. She would take a quick swipe at the cut and back off, she decided. As soon as she approached, though, the cow sensed her presence. She lifted her tail and delivered a stinging swat to Erin's arm.

"Oh!" Erin backed away, rubbing her arm.

Tyler laughed and she gave him an insulted look.

"You're going to have to hold her tail out of the way."

Erin looked at the long ropy thing. It looked like it had a whisk broom attached. Her hand came up slowly.

"Oh, quit looking like someone's trying to give you a handful of plutonium. Grab the damned thing, but don't break it off."

Erin's hand sprang away. "It's breakable?"

He rolled his eyes. "Well, not like Haviland china, but yeah."

"Have you ever broken one off?" She had a mental picture of a herd of tail-free cows trying to swat flies off themselves by switching their rumps back and forth.

"Nah," Tyler said. "It takes a lot of strength to do it."

"Which I probably don't have," she said indignantly.

"Probably not."

"Then why did you mention it?"

"It was just a warning."

Erin turned and gingerly grasped the cow's tail. It felt like a living rope. Grimacing, she moved it out of the way, swabbed the cut and sprang away.

"There," she said briskly. "All done." She put away the disinfectant and returned to the truck.

Tyler gave her a considering look. "You might make a proper ranch hand yet. You might just learn a few things if you stick around for a few weeks."

Erin gave him a quick, sideways glance. She suspected she would learn a great many things, and not all of them about cows.

She recalled her firm determination to pretend that the kiss had never happened. She could do it. Piece of cake.

NEVER HAPPENED? Good grief! What had she been thinking? Erin was still mulling the kiss over a week later as she vigorously scrubbed the fronts of the dismal green kitchen cupboards. The kiss was between them as clearly as if someone had deposited a boulder in the middle of the living room.

She couldn't escape thoughts of it. Thoughts of Tyler.

It had been seven days since the two of them had been sprayed by the skunk, six since their kiss at the hot spring. She had stuck to her decision to treat Tyler with the utmost professional courtesy, do the tasks he assigned her, and not think of him in any personal way. As a result, he looked ready to bite nails in half and she was as nervous as a cat locked in a kennel.

On reflection, she realized it had been easy for her to decide to be cool, courteous and professional. That had been before she'd spent her nights sleeping in the room down the hall from his.

At Mornfield Manor, she'd had her own quarters near the kitchen. She'd rarely even seen the Mornfields until they'd come, fully dressed, down to breakfast, ready to discuss with her their day's itineraries, the week's menus, or her tasks and errands. She'd liked it that way.

She didn't like the way things were with Tyler. It would be so much easier on her if he came into the kitchen fully buttoned up, dressed, shaved. Instead he got up early, while it was still cool outside, and started work. In spite of his statement that he needed a ranch hand, he stubbornly insisted on doing most of the outside work himself.

She was up, showered and dressed by the time he wandered in looking for breakfast and his first cup of coffee, usually with his shirt unbuttoned and his jeans riding low, hair tousled and jaw roughened by beard stubble. He looked messy, earthy and sexy.

It was more than any red-blooded woman should be expected to take.

As promised, Tyler had returned to using the crutches, or at least one. He could get around fairly well, though Erin thought his leg must hurt more than he let her see. He'd had to return to the crutches, of course, since she'd wrecked the wheelchair.

She still winced at the memory of that accident, and the stunned looks of the hospital personnel when she'd returned it and paid for the damage. She was never going to get out of debt at this rate, she thought, taking a swipe at a streak of dirt on one cupboard door.

In spite of the conflicts between them, Erin had to admire Tyler for how much he could accomplish with only one free hand. He was determined to do as much as possible on his own. She had never met a more stubborn man.

He was stubborn about locating his missing cattle, too. He'd called the sheriff, who'd sent out a deputy to investigate. The officer had been no more successful than Sam and Tyler in locating the missing animals. Tyler was clearly concerned, but he didn't talk about it much. He kept things to himself. Erin tried to tell herself it didn't bother her. After all, she was only a temporary employee. It wouldn't have bothered her with anyone else, but it was different with Tyler. Though she'd like to ignore it, she had an emotional connection to him, an attraction that grew by the day.

She had decided that either the encounter with the skunk truly had done something to her sense of smell, or there was something wrong with the air circulation in the house. Tyler had devised a way of covering his cast with a couple of large plastic trash bags to protect it while he showered. The system seemed to work well for him so he showered a couple of times a day—after breakfast and before dinner. While Erin appreciated his cleanliness, she'd discovered that the house always seemed to smell like his soap, shampoo, aftershave. She'd given the house a thorough cleaning. It should have smelled like the lemon-scented cleaner she'd used.

Erin paused to pick up the bottle and take a sniff.

Her eyes watered. It contained ammonia and was strong enough to knock over one of Tyler's horses. She frowned at the writing on the bottle. The house wasn't redolent of "lusty lemon scent." It was redolent of lusty Tyler Morris.

It was driving her nuts. She smelled him whenever she was working around the house. His scent assaulted her the moment she walked in from outdoors. She would have set around bowls of potpourri to counteract it if she'd thought he wouldn't toss them out.

Her emotional reaction to the situation had been to pitch in and begin doing what she did best: cleaning, organizing, tearing through cabinets and cupboards as if she were a tornado, leaving order in her wake. She loved it. Tyler hated it, but he hadn't stopped her.

Today, she intended to start on his office.

He was in the barn, washing down and grooming the mares. She'd offered to help him, but he'd refused, saying he liked to do it himself. She liked it, too, liked working with him, listening as he spoke softly to the animals. His voice had gentled her own fears of being around them. She felt secure with them now, comfortable in caring for them. But he didn't want her there, so she'd stayed inside.

She tried not to take it personally. Besides, she'd been itching to start organizing his office. She took one last swipe at some smudges on the refrigerator door—they were exactly the size of Bucky and Earl Junior's hands—picked up her cleaning supplies and headed for Tyler's office.

She grimaced at the mess of papers piled on his desk. They needed to be filed. She opened the top drawer of his file cabinet to see what kind of system he used and stared in dismay at the mess she found there. She had barely reached for the first folder when she heard the distinctive thump and bump of his feet on the hardwood floor.

"Lift your hands away from it," he ordered. "Turn around, and walk away."

She gave herself credit for not jumping and whipping around guiltily. Instead she lifted her chin as if the sight of him looming in the doorway didn't intimidate her, and glanced around. "You don't have to make it sound as though I've got one hand on a stick of dynamite and the other on a blasting cap."

"You might as well have," he said, stomping into the room. "You'll do about that much damage to my files." He brought with him the scent of hay, the mane and tail shampoo he used on the mares and fresh desert air.

Erin's knees weakened, but she stood straight and locked them. She was a strong woman. She could take it.

Getting her mind off how sexy he looked and smelled, and back on the conversation, she blinked at him in amazement. "How could they be any more damaged? You couldn't find anything in here. It's a mess."

"I like it that way."

"Tyler, you've got to be kidding. I helped devise an excellent filing system for Lord Vincent. Let me adapt it for your use."

His chin thrust out belligerently. It still looked smooth and shiny from his morning shave. Erin's heart butted against her rib cage, but she swallowed hard and dragged her attention back to the irritation snapping in his eyes.

"Will you pray tell me what the hell my records of cattle sales, vet bills and artificial insemination techniques would have in common with some English lord's trips to his tailor and his hairdresser?"

"Tyler, Mornfield Manor had a small, working farm on the property...."

"No." The statement was flat. Unequivocal. He took a long, patient breath. "Erin. I didn't stop you when you organized the kitchen cupboards. That's your job and I figured it would keep you out of trouble. I thought putting the spices in alphabetical order was a little obsessive, but, hey, everyone has their quirks."

"Thank you so much," she muttered, resenting his "woman's place is in the kitchen" attitude.

"Even though I can't find my favorite coffee cup, I don't complain," he added in a grumpy tone.

"Your, uh, favorite coffee cup?" Erin asked, not quite meeting his eyes. "That wouldn't be the one with the cracks around the rim and the bucking horse on the front?"

His eyes narrowed. "You know something about it?"

She grabbed a dust rag from her bucket of supplies and began to polish a geode paperweight.

"Erin," he said, dragging her name out in a warning tone.

Oh, heck, she might as well confess. "I threw it away."

"You what?"

She lifted her hands innocently. "How was I to know it was your favorite?"

"The fact that it was well-used?" he suggested. "What about my brown hat?" he asked suspiciously.

"The one with the holes, the crumpled brim and the nasty stains around the crown?"

"Honest sweat," he said.

She winced. "Be comforted by the fact that the cup and the hat are resting in peace together at the bottom of some landfill."

He lunged across the room and she jumped backward.

"You threw away my hat?" he demanded. "I wear it for branding. It's my favorite."

"Not anymore," she said feebly.

"You threw away my hat," he said faintly, as if he couldn't believe it. His deep brown eyes rolled heavenward as if asking for confirmation. "You threw away my hat. It was 10X beaver. Is nothing sacred to you?"

"Apparently not." What could she say? It had been old and ugly. She couldn't imagine that anyone would want it, not even him. Once again, she'd been wrong.

"What the hell kind of butler are you, anyway? Butlers are supposed to do what the employer says and nothing else, to be seen and not heard," he ranted.

"I think that refers to an old-fashioned idea about raising children," she said correcting.

"And you talk back!" he said wildly. "I never saw a butler before who talks back as much as you do—or at all for that matter."

She never had before. It would have gotten her fired, but things were different at the Morris Ranch. Somehow she couldn't seem to maintain the proper attitude of respect. She continually seemed to be wading into trouble, guns ablazing. "Sorry," she said with an apologetic shrug. She eyed him for a moment. "For a cowboy, you seem to know a lot about butlers."

He gave her a disgruntled look. "I'm learning fast. At lightning speed, in fact."

She answered with a sickly smile.

Tyler ran both hands through his hair, gripped his temples between his palms for a minute, then said, "Leave things alone. Don't throw anything away without asking, and get away from my file cabinet."

"I was only trying to help."

"Give me strength," he moaned. "I agreed to let you stay, Erin, but only to cook, clean and help me out around here. Leave everything else alone. Do you hear me?" He stepped back pointedly, obviously waiting for her to precede him from the room.

She lifted her chin in the air and walked past him, down the hall and into the living room with her back straight and her pride intact. She could hear Tyler coming along right behind her. "I was only trying to do my job...."

"Well, your job doesn't... What the hell?" His voice trailed off as he stared out the plate-glass window that gave a view of the driveway.

7

"WHAT IS IT?" Erin scurried over to see what was going on.

"Earl Junior's up to something," Tyler said, lifting his chin in a quick upthrust to indicate the boy. He was standing beside a fuel truck at the end of the driveway, talking to the driver. Once a month, the truck brought a refill of propane for the tank behind the house. It provided fuel for the kitchen range and the water heater. Junior seemed to be doing a great deal of shouting and arm waving as he pointed to the house.

"Don't jump to conclusions," Erin advised. "It might be perfectly innocent."

Tyler snorted. "And pigs can fly. I'd better go find out what's going on." He moved slowly toward the door, but by the time he reached the bottom of the front steps, the truck had taken the back road around the house and Earl Junior was skipping up the driveway to Tyler. Curious, Erin followed along.

"Junior, what have you been doing?" Tyler demanded when the boy approached.

He blinked guileless blue eyes. "Nothin'. I was just tellin' the new driver where to find the propane tank."

Tyler's eyes narrowed. "Since when did you get to be so helpful?"

The boy stuck out is bottom lip and scuffed his toe in the dust. "I was just tryin' to be good. You're always sayin' I cause trouble."

He looked so hurt, Erin's heart went out to him. "Tyler, don't be so hard on him," she murmured.

Tyler answered her with a disgruntled look. "Okay, Junior. Thanks for telling him where to find the propane tank," he said gruffly.

"That's okay." The boy turned away, then looked back over his shoulder. "If you wanna know, the driver doesn't hear too good. You have to yell and wave your arms around or he won't know what you're saying."

"Thank you for telling us that," Erin said, stepping in front of a still-suspicious Tyler.

Earl nodded and headed back down the driveway, but darted to one side and into some hackberry bushes.

"He's probably looking for a rabbit to torture," Tyler speculated morosely.

"Why do you always think the worst of those children?"

"Because that's all I ever see."

"They can't be all bad."

"You sound like Shara," he said, turning to go around the house.

Erin couldn't think of a reply to that, so she followed in silence. When they arrived around back, they saw that the driver had finished refilling the tank and was winding the hose back into position on the side of the truck. He nodded when he saw them and approached with a clipboard in his hand.

"*I need you to sign this invoice,*" he bellowed,

waving his arms and making writing motions with his hand.

Startled, Tyler stopped and Erin stumbled into him. They exchanged a look, asking each other if this guy was all right.

"I guess he thinks everyone else is hard of hearing, too," she whispered.

Tyler nodded, then yelled back. *"Okay."* He lifted his hand and pantomimed writing his signature. *"I'll be happy to."*

The driver jumped in surprise, gave Tyler a puzzled look, then handed over the clipboard. *"Right here."* He indicated the line where Tyler was to sign. He cupped his hands around his mouth and leaned close. *"Would you like me to read you what it says?"*

Tyler imitated the man's actions until the two of them were inches apart, bawling into each other's faces. *"Why would I want you to do that?"*

The loud voices startled a covey of quail, which dashed from beneath a creosote bush and scurried, chirruping in distress, into the desert.

The driver, a short young man with a shock of black hair, gave Tyler an apologetic look. *"Sorry. The kid said you were touchy about your hearing loss and about not being able to read."*

"Whaaaat?" Tyler gaped at him. *"If you're talking about that blond kid, he's a little con man who's about to get his butt spanked. He told me you're hard of hearing."*

"Huh?" The driver lowered his voice. "You mean you're not deaf?"

"No," Tyler answered in a furious tone. "And I guess you aren't, either." He took the clipboard, signed his name with a fast scrawl, shoved it back into the man's hands and turned to look for Junior.

"Nuh-uh." The man scratched his head as he gave them a mystified look. "Now why would a kid go and say something like that?"

Tyler frowned at Erin, then looked over to where they could hear rustling in the underbrush, followed by muffled guffaws. "Because he's perfectly innocent and I'm too hard on him."

"Huh?" the driver said again.

"Never mind. Thanks for coming out. I'll see you next month."

With a nod, and a look that asked if the people around here were a little light on the top deck, the man swung back into his truck and drove away.

"Erin, where's my rope?" Tyler asked loudly, looking around. "I need it to rope up a varmint and tie him to the fence post, only this time, you're not going to untie him."

A squawking noise in the bushes was followed by Earl Junior erupting into the yard. He gave Tyler a frightened look, but when he saw there was no rope in sight, he broke into gales of laughter and scampered around the house, no doubt heading home to tell his little brother of the trick he'd pulled on them.

"The little brat," Tyler muttered. "The only future I see for him is behind bars." He turned to Erin. "I guess that proves that... What are you laughing about?" His eyes narrowed suspiciously.

Erin's own eyes were overflowing with tears from the laughter she was choking back. "Nuh...nothing. Not a thing."

He loomed toward her. "You're laughing at me."

She pinched her lips, swallowed hard and widened

her eyes. "No...no sir, not me. Wouldn't..." A chuckle erupted. "Wouldn't think of it."

"Laughing at the boss isn't a very butlerish thing to do," he said pointedly. The irritation in his dark eyes began to lighten. When she would have stepped back, he reached out with his crutch and placed it behind her knee to hold her in place.

"You keep saying you don't want a butler," she said, giving up the fight to hold in her laughter and grinning at him, her eyes full of mischief.

"Especially not one who laughs at me." His hand came out to grasp her arm. He hauled her to him so that she bounced against his chest. Her hands flew up to steady herself, her fingers digging into the hard muscles of his shoulders. The intent look in his eyes had the humor draining from hers. The mirth that had bubbled through her was replaced by sexual awareness and excitement that sent her heart thrumming against her breastbone.

"You're going to have to apologize for laughing at me." The pressure of the crutch against the back of her knee, and the strength of his hand on her arm told her if she tried to escape, she'd land on her backside in the dust.

"Now, Tyler, you have to admit it was pretty funny—the two of you standing there bellowing at each other."

"I don't have to admit any such thing." He brought her so close she could see each of the long, black lashes that rayed out from his eyes, and the fine lines that crinkled at the corners. "But you have to apologize."

"I do?" Her eyes tried to focus on his, but instead, drifted down to his lips, which curved slightly.

"Yes, let's hear it."

"What'll happen if I don't?" she hedged. She was playing with fire, but somehow she couldn't stop herself.

Tyler brought his lips to within a breath of hers. "Are you sure you want to find out?"

Erin looked into his eyes, into the depths of his determination. She knew what he intended to do—if she would let him. He would kiss her and it would lead to far more than she was ready for. Her good sense snapped suddenly into place. "No," she said faintly, then again with more force. "No. I don't want to find out."

Turning, she left Tyler blinking after her in surprise. She hurried into the house, back to the task she'd started before Tyler had found her, forgetting that he'd forbidden her to touch his files. Shakily she opened a drawer in the file cabinet and began removing folders, giving them a cursory glance as she sorted them into piles on his desk.

She shouldn't have let him touch her. Whenever he did, she felt her resolve weakening. She had thought her determination was as strong as a concrete block, but now she knew it was as weak and crumbly as piecrust. This couldn't go on, she thought as she opened files and sorted bills into piles. She would be here for at least another month. Surely she could stay away from him, maintain her professionalism for that long.

"I thought I told you to leave these alone," Tyler growled from the doorway.

Erin jumped and whipped around. She gave him a guilty look, but decided to cover it with bravado.

"Yes, you did, but I know that once you see how my system works, you'll like it."

"No," he said furiously. "I won't."

She threw her hands in the air. "Why are you so stubborn?"

"Years of practice. Now leave this stuff alone."

"Ty, you're talking like a bastard," Sam Wettig said from the doorway. "You'd better apologize or she's never gonna marry you." When the two of them turned to him, he shrugged. "I knocked, but you were arguing so loud, you didn't hear me."

"She's been messing with my stuff," Tyler said resentfully.

"He's unreasonable," Erin said, shutting the file drawer by giving it a mighty shove with her elbow. She looked at the mess on the desk. Now that she'd started, she had to finish. She continued sorting while Tyler glowered at her.

Sam shook his shiny, bald head, strode into the room and thumped a stack of magazines down in the center of the piles of papers. Erin saw that they were more of what he'd been bringing around for three days now—bride and wedding magazines.

"I've been reading in these, all about the first few weeks of marriage and how you've got to talk the little things out before they become big problems that could ruin your marriage. The way you two are goin' at it, though, you're going to need a marriage counselor before you even get hitched." He shook his head as if he'd done his best with what he had to work with, but they weren't cooperating.

Tyler and Erin looked at each other. Their shoulders slumped in defeat.

"Sam," Tyler said doggedly. "We're not getting married."

"Well, of course not," the cowboy responded as if the two of them had lost their minds. "You don't have any plans made yet and I've been pushing you about it for a week now. Here," he said, picking up the magazine on top of the stack and handing it to Erin. "There's some nice weddin' dresses in here. Traditional. There's one that's kind of plain—white satin with seed pearls on the bodice that would be just right for you. Not too expensive, either. Page 57. I think you'll like it."

With a feeble smile, Erin accepted the volume from him. "Thanks, Sam," she said. He must have read the magazines carefully to have picked up a word like "bodice." Somewhere in the world there might be a more unusual wedding consultant than an ex-rodeo clown turned rancher, but she couldn't imagine what it might be.

Eerily enough, his suggestions usually turned out to be right on target. The things he thought she might like were ones she truly did like. She'd loved his idea of being married at the community chapel up the highway. It was a pretty little brick building shaded by cottonwood trees thirty feet tall. She also liked his idea of decorating the inside of the chapel with swags of grapevines and native grasses tied with raffia, and of having the reception outside under the trees.

She glanced at the magazine he'd indicated and sighed inwardly. She didn't dare look at the dress he'd picked out. She'd probably fall in love with it. She gave Tyler a helpless look and he frowned at her.

Sam stayed for a few minutes, discussing ranch work with Tyler and promising to ride out that afternoon to check on the remaining cattle Tyler had pastured farthest from the house.

When Sam left, Tyler looked at her with irritation in his dark eyes. "Are you encouraging him in this fantasy life of his?"

"No," she answered hotly. "You started this, remember?"

"I did?" he asked indignantly.

"Yes, my first night here, you had the chance to set him straight, but you didn't, and now look what's happened."

"Well," Tyler admitted. "I didn't think it would go this far."

"It's gone way too far. He's your friend. You should tell him the truth—that we're not in love with each other, not even interested in each other."

Tyler harrumphed under his breath and walked out, leaning on his crutch.

Erin knew she wasn't the one to convince Sam. Her hand stole over to flip open the magazine to the page with the dress Sam had recommended. She couldn't even convince herself.

"You don't stink near as bad as you did the other night, lady."

Erin looked around to see Bucky Breslin staring up at her. He was dressed in striped shorts and a denim shirt that was much too large for him. As usual, he had no shoes. His blond hair was uncombed, his nose was running and his mouth was rimmed with chocolate frosting and what looked like grape juice. Erin stepped back, putting the broom she'd been using on the back porch between the two of them. She'd been so involved in her task, she hadn't heard him open the screen door.

"You smell like a girl now," he added with a frown. He didn't sound as though he thought that was necessarily a good thing.

"Thank you," she said, then added. "I think."

Bucky looked around, his movements a little too casual. "Is Tyler here?"

Erin had quickly learned to be highly suspicious of this little boy. Earl Junior hadn't been around in the week since he'd pulled his trick on Tyler and the propane truck driver. The respite had been wonderful.

In a wary tone of voice, she said, "Tyler's in the barn. Why?"

"Just thought I'd go visit him." Bucky put his hands behind him and rocked back on his heels as he surveyed the place. His gaze flitted over the washer and dryer. Erin could see him mentally dismiss them as being too big and heavy to steal. Next he looked at the row of cleaning tools she'd hung from nails on the wall. Uninteresting, except for the feather duster. She knew he viewed it as a potential torture device to be used on Earl Junior, or possibly, on any available small animal. It scared her to realize she was beginning to understand the thought processes of this boy and his brother.

"You want to visit Tyler?" she asked, moving to block his view of the feather duster.

"Sure. Why not?"

Erin's eyebrows lifted skeptically. Bucky and Tyler never had "visits." Their encounters could best be described as run-ins, disagreements—the Battle of the Little Bighorn.

In the two weeks she'd been here, she'd witnessed several of them. Bucky and Earl seemed determined to make Tyler's life a living hell. Erin suspected that it was in reaction to their mother's interest in him.

Shara hung around a great deal, usually while wearing tight shorts and a cropped top. She spent her time at the ranch watching Tyler, watching Erin, but not watching her children. Erin wondered where she was right now. It was almost noon and Shara hadn't made her daily trip, swaying up the driveway on her spike heels.

"I'm not sure Tyler can visit right now," Erin said. "He's pretty busy."

"I won't get in his way."

That'll be the day, Erin thought as the little boy went down the steps and across the yard, scuffing up dust.

Erin watched him go, surprised by his mild-mannered politeness. Her previous encounters with him hadn't led her to suspect he was capable of it. She wondered if she should follow him out to the barn, just to keep an eye on things, but she knew Tyler wouldn't appreciate it if she did. He thought she meddled too much already. Besides, the two of them were doing a great job of avoiding each other. Why spoil things?

In spite of his objections, she had reorganized his office. When he got over being stubborn about it, he would realize her system was much more efficient. Right now, he was still at the point of stomping out of the office with a paper in hand, waving it at her, demanding she show him what the hell she'd done with the appropriate file, though that hadn't happened in the last couple of days.

Other than times like these, the two of them didn't talk much even though they ate breakfast, lunch and dinner together every day. Tyler had rolled his eyes at the precise way she set the table for each meal, at the way she served the food, but he didn't complain. Even he would have to admit that things had run more smoothly since she'd arrived—at least the house had.

Tyler hadn't said much about his missing cattle, though Sam had reported five more of them gone. The two men were clearly worried and Erin was concerned, too. Sharing Tyler's worries was becoming increasingly important to her, and she wished it wasn't so. After Sam's last call, Erin had seen Tyler standing and staring out the window toward Shara's house.

Surely he didn't suspect Earl Junior and Bucky of rustling cattle. The boys were hellions, but they were too small to make that many cattle disappear. She glanced toward the barn as Bucky slipped inside. On second thought, maybe she wasn't giving them enough credit.

She suspected that the two of them, or at least Bucky, had made an entire cake disappear yesterday. She'd baked one and set it on the kitchen table to cool. She'd planned to frost it after she'd finished polishing the woodwork in the living room. When she'd returned to the kitchen, it had been gone, pan and all, and she'd seen a little towhead, maybe two, bouncing down the lane, streaking toward home. She'd been irritated with the little brats, and even more so with their mother who refused to control them. She hadn't bothered to call Shara about the cake because she wouldn't have done anything about it. Besides, it was probably long gone by the time they reached home.

Erin carried the broom to the porch and put it away in the corner cabinet. She tried to accomplish the outside jobs Tyler gave her, but she was no ranch hand. She didn't mind feeding the horses or filling their troughs with water. In fact, she enjoyed it. They were beautiful, graceful animals and being around them gave her a sense of quiet and peace. She had quickly discovered, though, that shoveling horse manure was something she could live without.

She hadn't complained when Tyler had assigned her the task, however. Nothing could be as bad as dealing with the aftermath of a skunk attack.

Erin glanced out to the place beside the barn where Tyler had told her to bury her uniform and his shirt. Sardonically, he'd asked if she wanted to put a little marker on the place to commemorate the loss of her precious uniform. She'd told him she didn't need the uniform to do her job properly. That's when he'd assigned her to shovel manure.

A movement at the barn door caught her eye and Erin saw Bucky scurry out. A few seconds later, Tyler came to the open door and peered out, a puzzled look on his face as he watched the fleeing boy.

Bucky ran in a hunched-over position, his big shirt flapping in the breeze he created as he ran. Halfway down the lane, he stopped, did a little hop, slapped at his shirt and kept running.

Tyler looked over at Erin, who shrugged, telling him she didn't know what that had been about. He started to turn back to his work, but decided he needed something to drink. He adjusted his crutch under his arm and headed across the yard.

"Got any iced tea in there?" he asked, when she gave him a curious look. He knew she did. With a nod, she went to get some for him. He made his way to the base of the mulberry tree, sat down and rested his back against the trunk. He could have sat on one of the lawn chairs. She'd made a little arrangement with a small table between them. She had even found an old tablecloth, which she'd cut off and hemmed to fit, then anchored the cloth down with a vase she kept full of flowers. He'd scoffed at it, but he secretly liked it. He couldn't sit in the chairs, though, because they caused his leg to stretch out at an awkward angle, so he preferred the back steps, which were too sunny right now, or the patch of shade under the mulberry.

Tyler sighed and used his handkerchief to blot sweat from his forehead. Hell, he liked just about everything she'd done around here, and it was getting harder and harder to keep from telling her so.

He'd break his other leg before he would admit it, but once he'd figured out her method, he'd found her filing system to be very efficient and sensible.

She kept iced tea made fresh all the time because she knew he liked it. She'd learned about his incurable sweet tooth so now the freezer was full of cookies and other goodies she'd baked. All he had to do was put a few in the microwave oven and nuke them into warmth whenever he wanted some—when she'd let him. Usually she anticipated his cravings and had a treat ready when he walked in from outside. She couldn't seem to break the habit, training, whatever it was, of waiting on him. That wasn't what he wanted from her.

Erin came down the steps, handed him a glass of tea, along with a handful of peanut butter cookies, then sat beside him, her back against the mulberry, to sip her own. Naturally the rim of his glass held a sprig of mint, which she'd picked from a patch near the backyard faucet. It glistened with drops of water. He plucked it off and handed it back to her. Grinning, she accepted it, crushing the leaves between her fingers and carrying the spicy scent to her nose.

"You never give up, do you?" he asked, just so he could see the righteous indignation bloom in her eyes. This time it didn't, though.

She looked up, accepting the challenge he offered, and said, "There's a proper way to do things."

"So you've said many times."

"Then quit trying to get me to change."

Tyler paused for a minute. Was that what he'd been doing? He didn't want her to be different than she was. He'd hated it when his family had tried to change him. His aunt Eugenia was the only one who'd thought he should be himself.

Tyler lifted his knee, rested his wrist on it and dangled the glass from his fingers as he munched the cookies.

"What did Bucky want?" he asked.

Erin gave him a surprised look. "He said he wanted to visit with you."

"Visit with me? We never visit."

"That was my thought exactly."

"I didn't even know he was in the barn until I heard him leaving." Tyler sighed. "I wonder what he stole."

"What did you have in there that wasn't nailed down?"

"Not much."

Erin chuckled. "Same thing in the house. I think he and Junior stole a cake yesterday."

"What kind?"

"Fudge marble."

"Damn. My favorite."

"I know."

Tyler grinned and looked away, his gaze taking in the zinnias and periwinkles she was trying to grow in a flower bed she'd made around the back porch.

The cake didn't matter. Right now, nothing much mattered except this easy, meandering conversation between the two of them.

It kept him from concentrating on the fact that he was a man in torment. He wanted her so badly, he was tempted to forget his ethics and seduce her. It wouldn't be hard to do. He caught her looking at him in exactly the same way he looked at her—with lust.

He couldn't get away from her, though they didn't spend much time together. He smelled her everywhere in the house. That was why he'd begun going outside to work earlier in the day. She woke up early, showered early, so that the scent of her soap, lotion, shampoo, whatever it was, rolled down the hallway into his room, socked him in the nose and woke up his sex drive—not that it needed much to wake it up.

He'd caught a glimpse of her one morning going back into her room, her long curly hair wet and clinging to the back of her sensible robe. He glanced over at the no-nonsense bun that was twisted on top of her head. How he hated that thing. He wished she'd wear her hair down, but he wasn't going to ask. It would hint at his personal interest in her and that was the last thing in the world he needed to do.

This whole situation was more than any red-blooded American male should have to stand. His mind couldn't seem to concentrate on work, his hands itched to grab her, his lips wanted to kiss her, his hormones were screaming for relief.

"I'm afraid they're becoming uncontrollable," Erin said quietly.

"They sure as hell are."

"What are you going to do?"

"Pour this iced tea down my jeans," he sighed.

"What?" Erin whipped around to stare at him. "What are you talking about?"

He started. What had they been talking about? His eyes narrowed. "What are you talking about?"

"Bucky and Junior."

"Oh, yeah." He cleared his throat. "Me, too. I, uh, don't know what I'm going to do about them. They're not my kids."

"But they're on your property all the time," she said pointedly.

"Yeah, I know." Tyler finished his tea, rattled the ice in his glass for a second, then tossed it out onto the grass. Those kids caused Erin more trouble than they did him. He should explain about his friendship with their dad.

"I've known Earl Breslin for ten years," he said. "He's a good friend. Saved my life once when I got the bright idea that I could be a bull rider. I got thrown and almost stomped, but he and Sam pulled me out of the way."

"So you feel responsible for his wife and kids?"

"Yeah." Tyler looked at her, at the sympathy and understanding that drenched those green eyes. Sympathy and understanding for him, drawing more out of him than he wanted to tell. "He shouldn't have gotten married. Shouldn't have had kids, especially if he didn't intend to stick around and help her with them. Some of us aren't meant to have that kind of responsibility, to be parents." If she didn't hear the warning implicit in that statement, she wasn't as smart as he thought she was.

Her soft pink lips curved. "And some of you are," she said.

The woman was either stubborn or obtuse, he decided. He set his glass down and she did the same. He turned to her, determined to make her understand. "Now, listen, Erin…"

She stunned him by reaching out and grasping his hand lightly. "You can't tell me there's no chance this hand will ever change a diaper. You don't seem like a man who'd be afraid of a challenge like that."

He scowled at her. "Diapers are a minor responsibility in the whole fatherhood thing."

"You're afraid of responsibility? That'll be the day." She threw her hands wide. "Look at this place. You've got more responsibility than just about anyone I know."

"These are just things, and cattle.…"

"It's a business. You're a responsible, stable businessman."

He frowned at her. She wasn't listening. She wasn't taking him seriously. In fact, she was laughing at him. What was a man supposed to do? He turned toward her, put his arm around her and drew her close. "You don't listen too good," he growled and settled the argument by kissing her.

8

WELCOME, ERIN THOUGHT. Welcome back. His lips were hot and demanding. He'd meant to teach her a lesson, she knew, and he was, but probably not the one he'd intended.

He tasted wonderful, sweet and vital, and full of fire. He touched her with his tongue and she opened for him so he could share that sweet fire with her. He was generous, compelling, making her want more and more.

She was astonished to hear herself whimper in need, but wasn't surprised when he heard and answered her need by probing deep into her mouth. His taste was hot, spinning her senses with desire for him. The faint stubble of his beard brushed her skin, making it tingle. He smelled only faintly of sweat. Mostly her nose picked up the scent of soap—and man. Rough, tender, sexy man.

Heat rushed through her, making her breasts throb, her stomach clench, her womb flower with a warmth she'd never known before. It was sex. It was the most vital of basic instincts to mate. It was how nature had ensured the continuation of the human race. She knew all that, but this had nothing to do with science. She'd never felt this before.

His hands turned her, laid her down on the grass, gentled her, though she hadn't given a thought to protesting. Her hands went up and around his shoulders, diving into his thick black hair, kneading his scalp, his neck, his shoulders, skimming over his back to land at his waist. Excitement and desire shot through her when he pressed against her. She felt his hardness, his desire for her. She had to feel his skin. Her hands shook as she tugged his shirt from his jeans.

He pulled away, gulped, "God, Erin, what are you doing?" He didn't wait for an answer. His hands were busy unbuttoning her shirt, working the buttons through with fingers that were much steadier than hers. The front fastener of her bra followed. In seconds, her breasts were exposed to the air. To the sun. To him.

She felt a cool breeze on skin that moments ago had been covered by fabric, then felt the soft pressure of his hands, then the warm dampness of his mouth.

When his lips skimmed the top of her breast, she moaned. When they closed over the tip, she bucked, sending it deeper into the warm cavern of his mouth. Excitement and mindless desire consumed her. Frantically she lifted herself and curled around his head, kissing his neck, his shoulder, anywhere she could reach. Then her hands scrambled for the buttons so his nakedness could join hers.

"It's true," he groaned. "You're delightful." He strung kisses from one breast to the other. He lingered on one, returned to the first, put a line of kisses down her breastbone, ending at her stomach, ran his tongue over her navel. "Erin, I've thought about this. Dreamed about this. It's been hell."

"I...I know," she whispered shakily. "For me, too."

Tyler pulled away, sat up and started to jerk off his shirt. Though she could barely focus on him, she saw his eyes flicker upward. His curse split the air as he shrugged his shirt back onto his shoulders. He reached for her, sat her up as if she were a rag doll and pulled her bra and her shirt around her.

"What?" Erin asked, dazed. She gave him a confused look that had him leaning close to kiss her again. Her lips chased his when he pulled away, but he evaded her.

"Shara," he growled into her ear. "And the kids. Come on. Let's get you dressed."

"Oh, no," she breathed, looking around. She couldn't see them, but she knew he must be telling the truth. "I...I can't let them see me like this...I'll..."

"You'll sit still and let me straighten you out," he said firmly, forcing her to immobility by putting his hands on her shoulders. He looked into her eyes. "Damn," he breathed. "I'm sorry about this."

About what? Kissing her? Nearly making love to her? Or about being interrupted? She was too confused to make sense of it. Arousal didn't die in her as quickly as it seemed to have died in him.

Erin was touched by his awkward attempt to set her to rights, but her sense finally seemed to be catching up with her practicality. She pushed his hands away. "I can do it."

He sat back, buttoned and tucked in his own shirt, his eyes never leaving her flushed face.

It wasn't until Erin had her bra fastened and her shirt buttoned that embarrassment set in. She didn't have time to deal with it because Tyler gulped, shook his head and looked down at her, his dark eyes glittering.

"Are you all right?" he asked, examining her closely.

She wanted to say no. She wanted to demand that he forget about Shara and the boys and return to what he'd been doing, what they'd been doing, but she couldn't. She could barely form words.

"Ye...es," she stammered. "I'm perfectly all right. Why wouldn't I be?"

"Honey, I gotta tell you that no-nonsense butler tone of yours doesn't quite work when you've got whisker burn all over your face."

"Oh!" Her hands flew to cover her cheeks.

"Erin," he said, low and urgent. "I'm sorry to leave you, but I've got to go in the house for a minute."

"What?" She looked down. When she saw his arousal pushing against the zipper of his jeans, heat washed her face again. "Oh, I see," she squeaked.

"Yeah, well, so will our company. Stay here. I'll be back."

In an instant, he had pushed himself to his feet, hopped for a moment on his good leg while he collected his crutch, then was gone, and Erin was left alone. Gasping for breath, she tried to smooth her hair and clothes. Finally she pulled herself together and stood, picking up the two empty glasses as she did so.

Only then did she hear the commotion being made by the Breslin family. She saw that Bucky was heading once again for the barn. This time, he wasn't running, though. He was being dragged.

One of Bucky's arms was gripped firmly by his

mother, and under the other he held a tiny, mewling kitten. Earl Junior was running to catch up with his family. The eager look on his face told Erin he was anxious to see his little brother get into trouble.

Their appearance jolted Erin out of her embarrassment and dispelled the lingering desire Tyler had aroused.

"What's going on?" she asked.

Shara gave her son a disgusted look, then she glanced at Erin, and away. "Bucky took one of the kittens," she said as if she hated to admit it to Erin, of all people. Her eyes flickered to Erin again. "Now he's bringing it back."

"It wanted to go with me," Bucky insisted, his bottom lip protruding and his blue eyes full of angry tears. He sniffed, trying to keep them from falling. "It don't want to stay with its mama."

"Did it tell you that?" Shara asked in exasperation. Her gaze darted back to Erin, then away again, her heavily made-up eyes full of irritation and a hint of hopeless despair.

Why, she doesn't know what to do with him, Erin thought in surprise. She ignores her sons' behavior because she doesn't know how to deal with it.

Bucky didn't answer his mother. She sighed helplessly. For the first time, Erin felt sympathy and understanding toward her.

She heard the back door slam, then Tyler coming down the steps. She thought he must have recovered quickly, but she didn't dare spare him a glance to see. She was afraid one glance at him would make her blush, advertising what they'd been doing just before Shara and the boys arrived. She already felt as if her stubble-reddened cheeks made her a walking billboard.

"What's going on?" he asked. His sharp eyes took in the situation and Erin knew he'd quickly realized what Bucky had done.

Gently Erin reached out and took the kitten from the little boy.

With the little gray-furred body clasped carefully in her hands, she looked at Tyler and said, "Bucky took one of the kittens home to play with. He's bringing it back now."

The little boy looked up at her suspiciously. Shara frowned. Junior snorted like one of Tyler's young horses. "Didn't, neither," he said. "Bucky was gonna keep it, but it started cryin' and Mom heard it."

His little brother turned on him. "Shut up! You don't know nothin'!" He started to light into Junior, but Tyler stepped between them. Balancing himself on one foot, he used his crutch to keep them apart.

"Hold it," Tyler said. "You're not going to fight here. Junior, why don't you just mind your own business? Erin, take the kitten back to Sheba."

With a nod, she hurried away and did so, finding the nest Sheba had made for her family behind some sawhorses that Tyler used for saddle trees. Erin placed the kitten beside its mother, an orange cat with many scars who didn't look the least bit like a skunk. Sheba immediately leaped up to take charge, dragging her baby closer and licking it vigorously.

By the time Erin returned to the yard, the argument between the two little boys had heated up. They were yelling, Tyler was trying to keep them apart without being tumbled over himself and Shara looked ready to knock her sons' heads together. Before Erin returned to the group, Shara had pulled Bucky away and was shouting at him.

"You don't take things that aren't yours," she said. "You've gotta ask."

"Sheba don't care," Bucky insisted, giving his mother a defiant look. "She's got more babies."

His mother turned him slightly with one hand and drew her other one back as if she meant to spank his bottom, but Erin intervened by catching the other woman's arm. "Wait, Shara."

Everyone looked at her. It occurred to her that the four of them had been caught in the same situation she'd seen them in several times since her arrival. She'd bitten her tongue over Shara's neglect of her children, but she now saw that it was because of Shara's sense of hopelessness, not laziness or lack of love for the little scamps. Tyler, an only child, admitted he knew nothing about kids, but the fact that he tolerated the two boys, giving them chance after chance, showed he was willing to try. No matter what he said about not ever being a father, she knew he'd make a good one.

Now Erin smiled a brisk, professional smile, and said, "I think Bucky just doesn't know much about kittens, that they can't leave their mothers for several weeks after they're born."

Bucky opened his mouth as if to deny there was anything he didn't know, but Tyler gave him a stern look that kept him quiet. Man and boy looked back at Erin expectantly.

She wished she knew exactly what to say, but wasn't sure herself. With the others waiting for her, though, she soldiered on. "Maybe he needs a job."

"What kinda job?" the boy asked, intrigued.

"Making sure Sheba and the kittens are comfortable and have everything they need. Tyler could pay you to take good care of them."

Her boss raised an eyebrow at that suggestion but he didn't object. She knew it was like paying a hoodlum not to steal hubcaps, but it was the best she could do on the spur-of-the-moment.

"How much?" Bucky asked.

"How come he gets a job and I don't?" Junior broke in indignantly. "I'm older."

"Then you ought to be old enough to find a job that needs to be done, decide how much it's worth to you to do it and see if Tyler will pay you," Erin answered judiciously. "You never know, Bucky might think he can do a better job and do it for less."

"Nuh-uh, he can't, neither," Earl Junior objected, but she could see that the idea intrigued him. He immediately forgot about his argument with his brother, turned and began surveying the yard and the barn for possible employment. "I'll look for a job," he said, puffed up with importance. "Bucky can take care of those old cats. I can find a real job."

While Junior nosed around for something Tyler could pay him to do, Bucky asked Tyler how to take care of the cats, actually listening to Tyler's instructions about their need for a safe and quiet place, then tiptoed into the barn to be near them. A few minutes later, he emerged with an old pan that he rinsed and filled with water, which he carried back inside.

Shara looked after her sons, her face bemused. "You better hope Junior doesn't break something just so he can fix it for you, Tyler, and get paid to do it."

"I had the same thought, myself," he said, giving Erin a look that said he'd talk to her about all this later. He turned and slowly climbed the stairs into the house.

The women watched him go, then Shara turned to Erin. "Thanks," she said. "Sometimes I don't know what to do with 'em." Her full red lips parted in a grimace. "The truth is, I don't know what to do with them most of the time."

Erin knew she had to tread carefully with this woman. "It's hard sometimes," she said noncommittally.

"You don't know the half of it. I had 'em too young." Shara's hands lifted helplessly, her long red nails flashing in the sun. "I was just seventeen when Junior was born. I wanted to wait to have kids. I was just a kid myself, you know?" Shara shook her head, sending sparks of light through the bright tresses. "But Earl wanted kids right away, so we had Junior, and Bucky fifteen months later. Earl was glad, especially since they were both boys. I think he was just trying to prove how much of a man he was. Now he's off on the rodeo circuit, trying to win some money."

"But you need him here," Erin said sympathetically.

"Yeah, big time," Shara admitted. "I can't find him, though. I'm sick of him being gone all the time. I haven't talked to him in three weeks. I've called all the stops he's supposed to be making, but no one's seen him. That's why I've been thinking about…"

"Divorcing him?" Erin supplied.

Shara nodded and bit her lip. She looked away,

obviously ashamed of what she perceived as her disloyalty to her husband.

Erin was amazed that Shara would tell her something so personal, but she suddenly admired the woman because, in spite of her worries over Earl, she at least continued trying to care for her children. Earl wasn't even around to do that much. "It's hard to know what to do."

"Yeah, and the boys are too much for me. They're brats."

"I don't have kids, Shara, but I've been around lots of them."

"You have? I never was. I never baby-sat or did any of that stuff when I was a teenager." Shara rolled her eyes. "I was too busy hanging around the cowboys. I'd never even held a tiny baby until Junior was born."

"I've got several nieces and nephews and many, many cousins." Erin hesitated about giving child-care advice since she was clearly no expert, but Shara seemed to need all the help she could get. "One of my cousins, Diane, is the best mother I've ever seen. She's got two boys, like you do, and a little girl. Everyone loves having her kids around."

Shara shrugged. "Nobody likes having my kids around—not even me." She paused and gave Erin a sideways glance. "What does your cousin do that makes everyone like her kids?"

Encouraged by Shara's interest, Erin told her how Diane focused on her children, correcting their behavior firmly, consistently, but quietly whenever necessary, and always in private to avoid embarrassing the child. Shara looked interested, nodded thoughtfully, then went into the barn to check on Bucky and the cats.

Satisfied that she might have given a little bit of help, Erin started for the back steps. When she reached for the handle of the screen door, it opened for her. Tyler stood looking down at her.

"Giving child-rearing advice, Erin?"

"Why, yes," she answered coolly as she climbed the steps and walked past him. The look in his eyes told her the closeness they'd known a few minutes ago was as absent as snow in August. She wanted to know what was going on in his mind, to know what he was thinking, how he felt. How he felt about her. She still tingled from his caresses, but the closed look on his face told her it was the last thing on his mind. Well, a girl had some pride. She wasn't going to let him think she'd been affected by his lovemaking, or by his cool distance now. "As a matter of fact, I was," she said.

He leaned against the doorjamb, watching her as she walked past. "Is that part of your butler training?"

"We're trained to give practical advice whenever necessary."

Tyler grinned and let the door slam behind her. "I just love it when you get that Mary Poppins tone in your voice. Makes me think I ought to be put in my place."

Too bad it didn't work, she thought sourly.

"Shara seems to need help," Erin said.

"No kidding, but I still find it hard to believe it's part of your butlering job."

Erin's lips pinched in irritation. "I don't really

have a butlering job here, remember? You don't want
a butler.''

"That's right."

"So since this job doesn't resemble any butlering
job I've ever had, or even heard of, I'm making it
up as I go along, even to handing out child-rearing
advice. And if it helps you and gets those boys' behavior under control, why should you object?''

Tyler lifted his hand as if to ward off her anger.
"I wasn't objecting."

She clapped her hands onto her hips. The heck
with being cool and unflappable. She was no Jeeves.
"Then what were you doing?"

His devilish eyes laughed at her. "Getting a rise
out of you."

She gritted her teeth. "Your favorite indoor
sport."

His voice dropped to a low rumble. "It's not my
favorite, Erin, but it'll do until I can take part in what
is my favorite indoor sport once again."

She felt as if he'd slapped her, as if the moments
they'd just shared had meant nothing to him, been
cheap. Her heart clenched with the hurt she felt, then
anger rushed through her, painting her cheeks. "I
can't tell you how little that interests me," she said.

"Uh-huh," he answered, examining the color that
washed over her face. "I can see that." When he
said the words, Erin saw a flicker in his eyes as if
he didn't mean them, but she told herself she was
being a fool.

Back straight, head in the air, Erin turned and
strode into the kitchen. She expected his mocking
chuckle to follow her, but he was silent.

Tyler watched her go. Hell's bells. Why had he

said that? Hurt her that way? He rubbed his fist against his forehead in frustration.

Because he wanted her, had almost taken her, and it scared him worse than anything ever had. He knew somehow that if he made love to her, forever after there would be a connection between them that nothing could sever. Since he'd left his parents' home, he'd made such a point of his independence, of needing no one, of depending only on himself, he'd thought it would always be that way. That would all change if he touched her again. He knew that and yet he yearned for her.

He should send her away. He could do almost everything for himself now except drive the truck and mount a horse. He was capable of a lot more than he'd thought; nearly making love to her under the mulberry tree was proof of that. He was getting a walking cast in a few days and then there'd be no stopping him. He should send her away.

He couldn't do it.

"What a hell of a mess," he muttered, going into his office and shutting the door.

"ARE YOU IRONING MY BOXERS?" Tyler asked, stalking into the kitchen.

Erin's heart cha-chaed its way into her throat, then settled down again. It happened every time she saw him unexpectedly. She was beginning to think she needed to see a cardiologist. "Oh, hi. I thought you and Sam went into town to the feed store."

His face darkened furiously. "We did. We got the sulfur tablets. You'll have to help me put them out later."

Erin nodded. She knew he mixed them with the

feed supplements he gave his cattle. It helped them resist attacks by ticks. "You're usually gone longer," she commented. And darn it, she missed him every second he was away.

"I made Sam bring me straight home." Tyler frowned. "As soon as we finished at the feed store, he started talking about stopping at Ellie's Dress Shop."

Erin bit her lip. "Whatever for?"

"They rent tuxedos there," he said shortly, his furious look daring her to say something.

"Oh" was all she could manage to say before turning back to her work. She had to fight down a laugh. At last, she was no longer being singled out for Sam's advice on wedding attire. He had plans for Tyler, too, for this never-to-be wedding.

"I know what you're thinking," Tyler said. His new walking cast thumped on the floor as he moved across the room to the coffeepot. He got around extremely well on it and should be free of casts, and of her, in another three weeks.

"You couldn't possibly," she said in a choked voice.

"You're thinking that since Sam's my friend I should be able to get this crazy idea out of his head." Tyler clattered the coffeepot back onto its hot plate. "Well," he said, scowling into his cup before taking a drink. "I can't. I've tried, and I can't."

"I see." Erin wished he didn't sound so appalled at the idea of marrying her. Since the day he'd kissed her, been on the verge of making love to her, she'd begun entertaining hopeless fantasies of a life with him.

Tyler focused on her task once again. "Why are you ironing my boxer shorts?"

She had the ironing board set up, a stack of clothing on the table, the radio tuned to a country station—the only station in town—and was busy pressing a crease into his gray-striped boxer shorts.

He didn't like it when she worked in his bedroom, but she felt it was part of her job to organize everything in the house if she could—or maybe she was turning into a voyeur, unable to keep her fantasy life under control. It now extended to giving careful attention to his underwear. She was hopeless.

"Yes," she said cautiously. "I am."

"Why?"

"Because they lie more neatly in the drawer when they've been ironed, and because they fit more smoothly under your, uh, clothes." She was not going to look at his behind, or at that enticing bulge in the front of his jeans—nice though they were. She folded the pair she'd finished ironing, placed them on the table and looked at him.

"Erin," he said, exasperated. "I don't care if they fit neatly in the drawer, or neatly on my butt. I don't wear them. You've washed every pair of jockey shorts I own since you've been here. I thought you knew I didn't wear boxers."

"Then why do you have them?"

"Because Aunt Eugenia gave them to me and she has a habit of asking after every gift she's ever given me to make sure I like it, use it, will never part with it." He moved to the counter where the cookie jar sat and grabbed a handful of chocolate chip cookies.

Erin felt a surge of pleasure when he did so. He might preach at her about the fact that she was only there to help with the ranch work, but she noticed he didn't balk at the food she cooked, and the cookies she kept prepared to satisfy his sweet tooth. She gave him a critical look. He'd probably put on five pounds in the month she'd been at the ranch. In all the right places, too.

"Well, in that case, once they're ironed, they'll fit more neatly in your drawer." She picked up another pair, this one with a black paisley design on it, and began wielding her iron once again.

"I don't care about the neatness of my drawers," he said, beginning to do a slow burn.

She gave him a dismissive glance. "That much was obvious."

"Until you straightened them out."

"That's my job." She finished the front, flipped them over and began on the back.

Tyler watched her small, efficient hands, one smoothing and tugging the fabric of a pair of underwear he never wore, the other whipping the iron around as if she was a little kid with a toy race car.

He remembered what it had felt like to have those hands on him, skimming over his skin, drawing him close, fulfilling at least some of his fantasies.

Watching her was driving him crazy. He'd been doing it ever since she'd come. He'd never intended to let her stay, but she'd stayed. He'd never intended to let her take over his house, but she had. He'd never intended to let her polish, perfect and organize it. It was his house, after all, and he'd liked it the way it was. Maybe he hadn't been too fond of the dust balls under the bed, but they weren't doing any real harm, so he'd left them alone. She couldn't seem to leave anything alone.

Except him. There had been no more of those wild kisses, near-lovemaking episodes, and he wished there had been. In spite of his resolve, his knowledge that if he touched her again, he'd never be able to let her go, he'd give just about anything, even the belt buckle he'd won for bronc riding five years ago, if she was the kind of woman who wouldn't object to some freewheeling, no-commitments, get-it-out-of-our-systems sex. If she was like that, it would be easier for him to make love to her and let her go.

He rubbed his knuckles across his forehead in frustration and continued in a grim voice. "Okay, just for the sake of argument, let's say that is part of your job. Doesn't it strike you that this whole butler thing is a little outdated?"

She drew back. "What do you mean?"

"I mean look at what you're doing—cooking, cleaning, ironing. You've set the women's lib movement back thirty years."

She raised an eyebrow at him. "Like most men, you missed the whole point of the women's lib movement. The idea was that women should be allowed to do exactly what they like and are suited for in their lives and in their careers and get paid exactly what a man would get paid." She shrugged. "Butlers are much more than servants, nowadays, Tyler. They're administrators, sometimes of huge estates. Mornfield Manor, where I worked before, had twenty-seven rooms. I like this job, I'm suited for it and I get paid like a man."

He looked at her mouth, then skimmed his gaze over her body. He could think of several other things she was suited for. He shifted as he realized his jeans were beginning to feel tight. He went around in a perpetual state of semiarousal these days. Cold showers were becoming a permanent part of his life.

He bit into a cookie, then stopped to consider it. Maybe it was true that chocolate was a substitute, though a poor one, for sex. That must be why he was eating so much of it lately. "What about Shara?" he asked. "What's she suited for?" He'd thought he knew, but even that had changed since Erin's interference.

Erin tilted her head to the side thoughtfully. It drove him crazy because it arched her graceful neck in a way that made him want to plant kisses there. "We don't know yet. She's going into town today to talk to a job counselor. They'll test her skills." Nonchalantly Erin unplugged the iron and set it on the counter. "We're baby-sitting the boys while she's gone."

"Oh, God," Tyler groaned, then pointed a finger at her. "You've got that wrong. We won't be baby-sitting. You will. I'd think you'd have had enough of those kids. You were over there all day yesterday."

"Not all day."

"What were you doing, anyway?"

"We were discussing how to make her... wardrobe...more appropriate for job hunting."

"You intend to put a ten-inch ruffle on all her skirts?"

Erin's lips twitched. "I don't think we'll have to resort to that. She did have a few articles of clothing that would be appropriate."

"For work as a barmaid?"

Erin gave him a steady look, but she didn't answer.

Tyler had the grace to look ashamed. He cleared his throat, then asked, "Why does she want to get a job? She's never wanted to before."

"That's not true. She says Earl never wanted her to work, said she needed to be free to travel with him, only, of course, she couldn't do that once the boys started school, but even then, he had some notion about providing for her and the boys in a grand style. It sounds to me like he wants her to be some kind of decorative ornament."

Tyler knew that. Earl had always wanted Shara and the boys with him. Even when he was on the road by himself, he'd called almost every day. At least he had until recently. Earl was a possessive man. Since the day Shara had married him, he'd been afraid she would find someone else, which was why his recent failure to contact her was all the more puzzling.

"She's running out of money," Erin continued. "Her husband hasn't sent any in weeks. She can't even locate him."

Tyler knew that, too. He'd tried to contact Earl through friends on the circuit, but no one knew where he was. He'd left the circuit, saying he had some business to take care of, and dropped out of sight. Tyler was as worried as Shara was. He couldn't quite put a name to the feelings he'd had when he'd discovered that Earl wasn't following the rodeo circuit, hadn't been seen in weeks. His gut twisted with dread whenever he thought about Earl. He'd depended on that feeling in his gut more than once and it had saved his life. Earl had big dreams of making money riding broncs, or worse, bulls, but Earl's true talent was with horses. He could be an excellent trainer of quarter horses if he'd settle down to it.

"Besides," Erin went on, "I'd think you'd want her to have a job. It will make her more independent, self-reliant."

Tyler couldn't argue with that. Even though he didn't quite understand why she was doing it, he had to admire Erin's willingness to help Shara, to take on those bratty boys. He frowned at her. "Is this interest in Shara another of your organizational...stunts?"

"It's not a stunt. I'm good at organizing things."

Tyler shook his head in frustration, but it was tinged with admiration. Though he'd groused at Erin for giving child-rearing advice to Shara, he'd noticed it had made a difference in the boys' behavior. Shara was trying to be more consistent in her discipline without resorting to spanking. He took another bite of cookie as he felt his spirits lift. Maybe those two wouldn't end up in juvenile detention, after all. Though there were moments, frequent moments, when he'd be happy to see them locked up, sometimes he actually liked the little stinkers. Bucky had taken his job of caring for Sheba and the kittens quite seriously, preparing a corner for her in the barn and blocking it off with bales of hay so the kittens couldn't escape. He had even tried catching a couple of mice for her, but Tyler had convinced him to let Sheba do her own hunting.

Earl Junior had said he could help with the horses, and had saved Tyler many steps by bringing him brushes and curry combs, buckets, soap and water. The boy had even held one of the mares while Tyler had doctored a gash on her leg, talking softly to her in a way that echoed his father's gift with horses. Tyler was grateful to see the change in them. He didn't have to worry quite so much that they were going to burn the place down. The changes were due to Erin's interference, her organizational skills. He was grateful for that, and yet the knowledge only made the conflict within him grow. It was becoming harder and harder to imagine life without her.

9

"I'M NOT GETTIN' SPIT'S worth of cooperation from you two," Sam complained. His boot heels thumped on the wooden floor as he stalked across the kitchen. He plunked the box he'd brought with him down on the table where Erin and Tyler sat finishing breakfast, then began searching through cupboards for a coffee cup. Finding one, he poured himself a cup of coffee and joined them at the table. He took off his cowboy hat and turned it upside down as he set it carefully on the table.

As Erin watched in amusement, and Tyler with an expression of dread, Sam spun a chair around and straddled it. He took a sip of his coffee, set the cup down, then flipped the lid off his box and dug his hand inside. When he pulled out a fistful of satin, voile and lace fabric swatches, Tyler groaned.

"Now, see," Sam said indignantly, tossing the delicate fabrics down on the table. "That's exactly what I'm talking about. This is the attitude I've been gettin' ever since we started this project. Do you think it's been easy for me to make these trips into town every day?"

"Uh, Sam, we didn't ask you to," Tyler said pointedly. "In fact, we'd prefer it if you'd just drop..."

"Do you think I like those strange looks I've been

getting at the fabric shop in town? Why people think I'm sewin' myself some women's underwear, or something.'' His homely face looked so hurt and indignant, that Erin reached over and squeezed his sinewy forearm.

"Sam," she said. "We know it's been hard for you, and we really appreciate all you've done, but—"

He waved his hand in the air to cut her off. "It's nothing. I'm glad to do it. Ty's my best friend," he said, giving Tyler a fond, but disgruntled look. "He deserves a nice wedding, though I'm beginning to think you're not the right bride for him. You're way too good for him," Sam admitted as he gave Tyler a long, considering look.

Erin giggled and Tyler glowered at her and Sam.

"You're at least giving me some cooperation." He gave her a sidelong look and she was amazed to see a hint of red paint his stubbly cheeks. "Liked that dress I picked out for ya', huh?"

As expected she'd fallen hopelessly in love with it. "Yes," she sighed, not daring to look at Tyler. "It was beautiful. It's exactly what I would want if I was getting married."

Sam didn't even hear her. "Told ya." He looked at Tyler. "And you. You won't even look at tuxedos, even after I said it would be all right if you wore your best boots for the wedding."

"Sam," Tyler said desperately. "Try to focus." He sat forward, placed his hands on the table and looked his friend in the eye. His face was as grimly determined as if he'd decided to shove his head through a wall and nothing was going to stop him.

"Listen to me and hear what I'm saying. There's not going to be a wedding. We're not getting…"

"Do you two just expect to run off and elope?" Sam threw his hands in the air and rolled his eyes as if appealing to heaven for help. "You know your aunt Eugenia would skin you, and so would your parents. It's bad enough you're not planning to run the family business like your dad keeps begging you to, but if you don't give them the pleasure of a nice wedding, they'll never forgive you."

Erin shot a quick glance at Tyler, but he didn't meet her eyes. She wondered what the family business was, but the stubborn set of his chin told her that if she asked, he probably wouldn't answer her.

The tension that had been in the house before had now become even more strained because of the sexual awareness that simmered between them. She went to sleep every night thinking of him just down the hall, longing for him. The fleeting fantasies she'd entertained about the two of them making love, living here together, were becoming a permanent fixture in her mind. They hardly spoke, even when they shared a table for a meal, as they were now.

They moved around each other warily, but she knew where he was almost all the time, was aware of him. They were only days away from the removal of his cast, from the moment she would be leaving. It didn't help that Sam showed up almost every day with some new idea for their "wedding."

Seeing that he was getting nowhere with Tyler, Sam turned to Erin. He spread the swatches out for her to see. "Have you been thinking about colors like I told you to?" he demanded.

Meekly she nodded, and threw another quick

glance at Tyler. She couldn't stop her fingers from straying toward the swatches and lightly rubbing the soft materials. "You're right, Sam. This periwinkle blue would be perfect for bridesmaids' dresses."

"Yeah, I read it's a color most women can wear." He picked up the voile, which was printed with a faint impression of multicolored tulips. "And wrap some of this around the brims of big, picture hats. Or white cowgirl hats. That would work. Mrs. Simpson, in town, can make the dresses for you if you want. She's a seamstress. I got her name from Ellie Redding at the dress shop."

Tyler clapped his cup onto the table. "Sam, where the hell did you learn all this stuff? Colors and fabrics and the right kind of candles for the reception. You never gave any of this a minute's thought in your life."

"Never had a reason to," Sam answered. "My best friend was never gettin' married before."

"Well, isn't it customary for those things to be left up to the bride and groom?" Tyler asked testily.

Sam leaned across the table. He looked Tyler in the eye and spoke in a tone of voice that indicated his friend wasn't too bright. "And I would do that, too, if it looked like you two were doing anything along that line yourselves, but you aren't doing a blessed thing."

Tyler took a slow, patient breath. "That's because we're not getting married."

"'Course not. You haven't even set the date."

"That's because there's nothing to set the date for," Tyler put his head in his hands and talked to the tabletop. "We're not getting married."

"Then you'd better talk to Reverend Martin. I told him to expect your call."

"Why did you do that?" Tyler asked helplessly.

"Because neither of you thought of it."

With another groan, Tyler leaned over and rapped his forehead against the tabletop.

Sam just shook his head. "Reverend Martin offers counseling to engaged couples and to tell you the truth, I think you two could use it. I think you've been fighting." He sat straight, crossed his arms on the top of the chair back and looked at them as if he was expecting confirmation of his suspicions.

"We haven't been fighting," Erin said quickly. She knew it was a vain hope that he would drop this subject. He hadn't dropped it since the minute they'd met and he'd decided she was the girl for Tyler. She gave Tyler a longing glance. She wished he could see things that way.

"You don't even look at each other much, at least not when I'm around," Sam went on. "But when you think the other one's not looking, you both have faces like a couple of lovesick calves—just like you did right now, Erin."

Erin's gaze zipped over to Tyler, who lifted his head to gaze at her with a look as startled as hers. Her gaze bounced away. Oh, why couldn't Sam just shut up? Embarrassment burned inside her, coupled with excitement that caused her stomach to flutter ridiculously. Thinking about Tyler looking at her with the expression of a lovesick calf made her feel like a schoolgirl with her first crush.

When neither of them answered, Sam shook his head. "When can I tell Reverend Martin to drop by?

Or do you want to go to his office? He's flexible either way.''

Tyler, who looked as if he'd had enough, started to rise from his chair, a wild look in his eyes. "Sam, how much damage did that bull do to you, anyway? Why don't you listen? How can you get through life without ever listening?"

Sam stopped, gave him a puzzled look and said, "Listen to what?"

Tyler groaned for the third time and Erin said quickly, "We'll have to let you know, Sam. We can't make a decision about talking to Reverend Martin right now. We're very busy, and..." Her voice trailed off because she didn't know what excuse to make. There weren't many Sam would accept.

"Well, okay," he said reluctantly. "But you two had better get on the ball. It's about time to pick out wedding invitations."

When Tyler made another move toward his friend, Erin leaped up and rushed around the table to push him back into his chair. "We'll do that, Sam," she said brightly. "In the meantime, would you like more coffee?"

She whipped the pot off the hot plate, refilled everyone's cups and shoved a plate of sweet rolls at Sam. He took two and munched happily.

"By the way, Ty, have you heard anything from the sheriff?" Sam asked.

"No." Tyler seemed to have calmed down and Erin gratefully resumed her seat. "You haven't seen anything suspicious, have you?"

"Nah."

Tyler looked at his friend, and then at Erin. Her eyes lit with humor and he shrugged as a moment of

understanding rushed between them. She knew what
he was thinking. Sam was a good man, but obtuse.
She doubted he would notice if someone was running
cattle beneath his bedroom window.

Tyler drummed his fingers on the table. "It's
about time for him—or them—to hit again."

"How do you know that?" Erin asked.

Tyler pointed to the calendar. "Look at that. This
guy's hit me at the end of every week for a month
now, though always in a different section. Today's
Thursday. If it's going to happen, it'll happen Friday
or Saturday night."

"Are you going to tell the sheriff?"

"He can't watch my whole spread, or spare the
men to do it. No. I'm going to take care of this myself."

Erin glanced down at his leg. His removable walking cast allowed him to get around fairly well, but
he still couldn't ride. "How?"

"I'm going to bring all my cattle into a valley over
there on the other side of the hot springs and wait."

"Isn't that kind of obvious? Won't he, or they,
suspect something if your entire herd is gathered in
one place?"

"Not necessarily. I've got some branding to do
and some yearlings to fatten up and sell. I do it every
year about this time."

"And you think these rustlers know that?"

Tyler gave her a weary look, but something dangerous glittered in his dark eyes. "Yeah, I do.
He...or they knew I was laid up with a broken leg,
didn't they?"

The way he said it made Erin sit up straight and
stare at him. The rustlers knew him, knew what was

happening with him. Erin wondered if he, in turn, knew who was doing this to him.

Tyler turned to Sam and asked him to help out by gathering the remaining cattle in the valley. Sam promised he would, scooped up two more sweet rolls and ambled out the door.

Tyler stood, too. "Erin, I'll need you to drive me out to the valley with my gear and drop me off."

With calm efficiency, she began clearing the table. "I'll drive you out there, but there won't be any dropping off. I'm staying, too."

That brought him up short and he laughed in disbelief. His gaze ran over her jeans, neatly tucked oxford-style shirt and the secure bun on top of her head. "You? Have you ever camped out?"

"Of course. Have you forgotten the trip across Mexico on a Honda?" No need to mention how she'd hated the discomfort of camping out.

He scowled at her. "That was a pleasure trip. This might be dangerous."

"You still can't get around very well," she said pointedly. "You'll need me."

"For what?"

"Whatever you can't do for yourself." The thrust of her chin matched his. She was pleased that she wasn't backing down from his irritation.

"Why are you so damned stubborn?" he demanded, grabbing his hat off the rack by the back door and slapping it against his knee.

"Because I work for the stubbornest man in the world. It rubs off."

He glowered at her for a moment longer, then turned away. "There are sleeping bags in these cupboards on the porch."

"I know. I aired them out last week and reorganized those cupboards."

"Why am I not surprised?" he muttered. "Since you seem to know so much, why don't you get things ready and we'll leave just before dark?"

She nodded and watched him go out the door, across the porch and down the stairs. He moved easily now, walking on his modified cast with a loose, swinging gait that gave her a hint of what he would be like in a week or so, when the cast would come off and he wouldn't need her anymore.

She could hardly bear the thought of leaving here. Of leaving him. She went along with him when he tried to convince Sam that they weren't getting married, but it hurt every time he said it and she felt as if she were the worst kind of fraud when she agreed with him. She knew it was true, but she didn't want it to be. She wanted to marry him, live with him here, have children with him someday.

She was in love with him. Hopelessly so.

The realization spread through her, finally making sense of the reactions she'd had to him since the day she'd walked into his house. She had wanted him to admire her efficiency, her cooking, her organizational skills, her achievements. Her. She had wanted it because she loved him and wanted him to love her in return.

How foolish of her. He'd never made any secret that he was a loner, had been a loner for years, and intended to stay that way. How could she have made such a mistake as to fall in love with him?

Agitated, Erin turned away from the door and hurried to the sink. She dumped in the dishes, added soap and water and began washing with quick, jerky motions that threatened breakage to the glassware.

The only solution she could see was to never let him know how she felt. Surely she could do that. She could keep on as she had been, maintaining a distance. It wouldn't be that hard. It wasn't as though Tyler exhibited a desire to be around her, to talk to her, confide in her, make love to her. He kept his distance. She could to.

"BACON AND EGGS," Tyler told Erin firmly.

"Why do you need bacon and eggs for camping out?" she asked in an exasperated tone that he didn't think he deserved. "You eat breakfast cereal or pancakes every morning of your life. Why go to the extra trouble of taking along eggs and bacon?"

"Wait'll you taste them cooked over an open fire," he said persuasively. "There's nothing like it."

"I'll bet." With a sigh, Erin went to the refrigerator, removed the requested items and added them to the cooler she was filling for their camp-out.

Satisfied, Tyler went into the bedroom for extra pillows. Ordinarily he wouldn't even use one, but he knew Erin would need them. She wasn't used to roughing it and he didn't want her to be bruised after a night on the ground.

His thick brows drew together in a frown as he thought about that. When had he begun caring that she not get bruised?

Tyler shifted his shoulders in an uncomfortable little shrug. Because he cared about her. More than he'd ever intended to. She belonged here, had a place here. He wanted her to never leave him.

He paused in the hallway and looked around, from the door to her room, which stood half open, to the door of his own, then his gaze skimmed along the wood panels of the floor and baseboards. Everything in the place was clean and dust free and it wasn't only because this was her job. He knew for a fact that there weren't too many domestic employees who took this kind of pride in their employer's home.

He'd caught her humming as she worked, though she probably hadn't been aware of it. He doubted that the fancy butler school she'd attended encouraged humming. She'd also been willing to tackle any outside job he'd assigned her, even shoveling manure. She'd hated it but she'd done it, first out of a sense of duty, then from a sense of pride. She liked the place to look good because she loved it here.

There weren't many things that could put Tyler at a loss for words, make him feel humbled and uncomfortable, but knowing Erin loved his ranch, his house made him stumble around to come to grips with his feelings. Men weren't supposed to have those, were they? Weren't they supposed to be strong and macho and leave the tender feelings to the women?

Tyler shivered and continued down the hall. Hell. When had he begun thinking about things like that? He stomped through the kitchen, pillows under his arm. Erin turned to give him a questioning look, but his frown told her not to bother. He saw her secretive little smile as she went back to her task and that irritated him further. Why did it always seem as if she knew what he was thinking?

"Are you ready?" he demanded when he had carried the camping gear out to the truck. "I want to get going."

''I'm ready.'' She snapped the lid on the cooler after she'd dumped ice on the bacon and eggs he'd insisted on taking and glanced up with a smile.

There she went again, looking as if she was laughing at him, but with gentle affection as if she knew what was going on in his mind. How could she? He didn't even know. He gave her one of the scowls that he used to keep her at a distance, then destroyed the whole effect by picking up the cooler and carrying it out for her, though his bum leg made it hard to balance. She followed along, carrying the small, overnight bag she'd packed for herself and locking the house behind her.

They finished loading the truck and started off. He admitted to himself that he admired the way she had forced herself to learn to drive his truck. He knew it was hard for a novice to handle, but after her initial experience, when she'd wrecked the wheelchair, she'd taken to it like a duck to water. She could drive it anywhere.

He sat back, gave her directions to the small valley and watched as she took him where he wanted to go. She drove with her back straight, hands gripping the wheel, eyes alert as if she didn't want to miss anything.

When they arrived at the valley, he was grateful to see that Sam had been true to his word and driven the majority of his herd in.

Tyler pointed to an area of palo verde and willow trees. ''We'll make camp over there. There's a wash behind it where we can park the truck. I'll cut branches to cover it so it won't be so noticeable.''

Erin gave him a teasing glance. ''Oh, yes, it should be easy to hide this thing.''

He grinned back before he could stop himself. Darn, why did she do that? He didn't know anybody who dared tease him the way she did.

When she stopped the truck, Erin looked around and said, "I didn't even know this was here."

"Only people familiar with the area know about it," he admitted, climbing down and looking over to where part of his herd had discovered the stream, which was thankfully running full of water. "I haven't used it often because the salt cedars were choking out the stream. I did a controlled burn last year and the grass is just now coming back. It's still ecologically fragile."

When Erin gave him a startled look, he grinned at her. "Don't look so amazed. Contrary to popular opinion, ranchers do take care of the land. If we didn't, we'd be out of business, and consumers would be out of beef."

She blushed—something he hadn't seen her do since the night they'd bathed in tomato juice. "Oh, well, I didn't mean that..."

"Yes, you did, but it's all right. Just don't buy into the popular myth that ranchers are destroying the land. Maybe some are, but most of us can't afford to."

She nodded and gave him that secret little smile that said he'd done something that pleased her. What had he done besides talk to her as if he cared what she thought? He did care, though he didn't want to. He'd been fighting this for weeks now, fighting to keep her from mattering to him. He'd decided long ago to be a loner because he couldn't imagine finding a woman who would want to share the uncertainties of his life, either with the rodeo, or now that he had his own place. Why had she come along to spoil all his firmly held notions?

They made their camp, but did without a campfire for fear of bringing attention to themselves—which showed how ridiculous it had been for him to insist on bringing bacon and eggs with them. He watched in surprise as Erin went about gathering up the long, needlelike palo verde leaves that were lying around thick on the ground. She mounded them for cushioning and spread their sleeping bags on top.

"How did you know to do that?" he asked, sitting against a tree and stretching his legs in front of him.

"Common sense."

"They didn't cover camping out in butler school?"

"It's probably an advanced class I'll have to go back for," she answered flippantly. She brought a thermos of coffee and two cups and sat down beside him. She poured some for both of them and handed him his cup.

Tyler sipped as he listened to his cattle settle down for the night. Dusk was his favorite time of day, especially if work had gone well. To his surprise, since Erin had come, he'd discovered that he liked having someone to share this time with. Liked having Erin to share it with.

He turned to her suddenly and said, "Erin, I've been hard on you since you came here."

She froze with her cup halfway to her mouth and looked at him over its rim.

He knew he'd surprised her, but he didn't give her time to respond. Now that he was talking, he might as well finish making a fool of himself.

"How much do you know about my family?"

"Nothing. Miss Eugenia never said anything about them."

"I'm an only child. My parents are rich. Very rich. I guess you could say that all their hopes were—are—pinned on me, but I had no interest in the family business."

"You wanted to be a cowboy," she said with a smile.

"My parents bought me a horse when I was six. An Arabian mare. She was beautiful, but it wasn't English riding, or dressage, or show horses I was interested in. I wanted to be in the rodeo." He told her how he'd left home at eighteen to follow the circuit and about his parents' fury. "They didn't speak to me for years," he added.

"That's why you've always been so close to Miss Eugenia," Erin suggested.

"They've been calling lately, my dad especially, wanting me to sell out, return home and begin learning the family business. He wants me to take it over, but he's got a whole army of vice presidents who would be much better at it than I am."

Erin nodded sympathetically. "You're a businessman in your own way, but I can't imagine you working in an office."

"Me, neither, but I can't convince him of that." Tyler paused. This next admission caused him the most worry. "I've thought my dad might have something to do with this rustling, trying to drive me out of business so I'd have to return home."

"Tyler, no. Not your own father."

He lifted a sardonic eyebrow at her obvious shock. "Erin, do you know who my dad is?"

"Well, no."

"He's Jonathan Morris of Morris Manufacturing."

It only took her seconds to understand what he was saying. "Morris Manufacturing is one of the major employers in this state."

"Plastics, microchips, yeah, it keeps a lot of people busy. It's a good living, but it's not for me and I hope my dad will accept that eventually. Aunt Eugenia says he will, but I'm not sure how well she knows him, even though he is her brother."

Erin was silent as she stared at him, her green eyes drenched with sympathy. He didn't deserve that from her.

He stared at her, unsure how to go on. "I acted like a bastard to you when you first came, not because of who you are but what you are. When I was growing up there were servants everywhere. We even had a chauffeur that drove me to kindergarten. Embarrassing as hell for a little kid."

Erin's green eyes were skeptical. "You're prejudiced against servants? I find that hard to believe."

"Nah. It's not that. It's the whole idea of having so much money, a life so busy with work and social obligations that you need people to help you handle things." He paused, recalling the harried life his parents had led. "It's being so busy you don't enjoy life." He looked over the small valley. Shadows were stretching across it, bringing darkness. Although he dreaded the coming night and the confrontation it would bring, he drew peace from the quiet scene.

Erin smiled at him. She set her cup down and reached over to place her hand over his. "Are you enjoying life now?"

"Yeah." He looked down at her hand, small and

pale against his. "It's been a lot more lively since you showed up."

She smirked at him, then said hesitantly. "Tyler, you don't really think your father has anything to do with the rustling, do you? Not your own father?"

"He can be ruthless."

"But not with his own son."

He gave her a considering frown, then shook his head. "No. I guess not. He wouldn't set out to hurt me." Somehow it had been easier to think his father was responsible than to consider the other possibility that had been growing in his mind.

"A father wouldn't do that."

He was touched by her naiveté, but puzzled by it. "How would you know? You don't know much about fathers. Aunt Eugenia told me yours abandoned your family when you were practically a baby."

He saw the shock run through her and he cursed himself as she drew away. "I'm sorry," he said, awkwardly reaching one hand out to her. "I'm a bastard to have said that to you."

Her voice was soft with hurt. "My father's leaving us was his loss, not ours. From what my mother said, Mark, Paul, Dave and I were lucky not to have known him, he…"

"Erin, I'm sorry. I always seem to say the wrong thing around you." His heart clenched with regret, a new emotion for him. "It seems I've had no sense from the moment you walked into my life. You've been driving me crazy."

That seemed to please her. The hurt drained from her face to be replaced by dawning anticipation and delight. "I have?"

"Yeah, and don't sound so happy about it." He put his own cup down, shoved it away and put both hands on her arms to draw her to him. Her eyes were fully open and bright with surprise. She couldn't be any more surprised than he was.

He was about to do something that they might both regret. But he had waited long enough.

10

WHEN TYLER REACHED FOR HER, Erin was battered by a combination of joy and fright. He wanted her. He might not love her the way she loved him, but he wanted her. What's more, he seemed to care about her, about her opinion of him. That's why he'd told her about his family, explained his reasons for his objections to her arrival, to her job.

Erin's love for him overcame her scruples and she went willingly into his arms. Heat from his hands seared her as they touched her face, her shoulders, then skimmed down her back to her waist. He looked at the places his hands touched, looked at her in a way no one else ever had before, with a passionate intensity that made her weak.

Gently he lifted her until they knelt, thigh to thigh on the soft ground. Trembling began deep within her. It was prompted by desire, need—and a lingering awe that he found her appealing.

Tyler drew her close enough that she could feel the evidence of his desire pressing against her. She started in excited surprise and he soothed her with gentle words.

"Easy, Erin. It's all right. I won't hurt you." His mouth murmured the words just millimeters from her own lips. She wanted to tell him that she knew he wouldn't hurt her, but when his lips took hers, she couldn't form a coherent thought. Whatever she'd been about to say didn't matter. Only kissing him, being kissed, touching, loving seemed to matter right now.

His fingers moved to unbutton her shirt, spreading it wide and slipping it off her shoulders. The warm July breeze swept across her bare shoulders and she shivered.

"You can't be cold," Tyler murmured against the skin of her throat. He skimmed kisses down to the hollow between her breasts.

"No," she moaned with pleasure. "Excited, scared."

"Don't be," he said, freeing her of her bra. "I brought protection."

"You planned this?" she asked on a laugh, holding him away.

His eyes glittered at her in the waning light. "Nah. I've been carrying it around for two weeks, wishing you were the type of girl who would be interested in a little recreational sex because I was going crazy wanting you. But you're not that kind of girl."

She smiled fondly. "I've got news for you, cowboy. You're not that kind of man."

He didn't answer, because he had her bare from the waist up now and he was taking a moment to admire the perfection of her breasts, the way they nestled into his palms, the peaking of her nipples as if they were begging for the touch of his mouth.

Bending, he kissed one, and then the other, then returned to the first and opened his mouth over it. When his tongue slid over her nipple, her body bucked against him, sparking his own arousal.

She was so sweet, so responsive, that he felt suddenly awkward, knowing that whatever he had to give this woman wouldn't be enough. It could be only sex, but the trembling of her hands when they reached for the snaps of his shirt told him it was far more than that for her. The thought that this might be love seemed to freeze all of his thought processes. He'd never known any feeling like this, so if it was love, it was completely new to him. When her small, efficient hands slipped beneath his opened shirt and kneaded his skin, he felt burned by her touch. He forgot about thoughts of love and concentrated only on needs.

When Tyler picked her up and laid her on his sleeping bag, Erin's heart nearly stopped. The downy softness closed around her, bringing with it the scent of the leaves beneath them. The warmth of the ground seeped into her back, but it was no warmer than his mouth as he tasted and tested her from her face to her shoulders, from her breast to her waist. He pulled the pins from her hair and spread it out around her head. "I've always wanted to see this," he admitted. "It's a sin to keep it up in that damned bun."

She smiled fondly at him and he kissed her again.

Tyler removed her shoes and jeans, then his own, along with the cast that was held by Velcro straps. Seeing him without it for the first time made her heart catch and her mind tumble with thoughts of leaving soon, but she pushed them away. This moment was for her enjoyment, and his.

Erin looked at him, then closed her eyes, sealing the sight of his strength and perfection into her mind.

Her hands lifted to draw him in as he knelt over her. Her arms went around his shoulders. "I've seen you without a shirt, but I didn't know you were this beautiful,'' she murmured.

He gave her a kiss that was full of tenderness. He ran his hand over her hip, savoring the softness of her skin. ''You're the one who's beautiful. I'm scarred and beat-up, and I've still got a broken leg—but I have no intention of letting it hamper my performance, if you know what I mean.''

She laughed. ''I have absolute faith in the strength of your performance,'' she assured him.

That laughing acceptance brought him to her then, to kneel before her, lean over and kiss her. She felt only him, was surrounded, intoxicated and finally, invaded by him.

She arched to meet him as he filled her. Unexpectedly, she felt tears swimming in her eyes because it was so perfect. Tyler was wrong. He was beautiful, and the way he made her feel was just as beautiful.

She had never felt this closeness before, this outpouring of love that welled up, filling her eyes with tears.

Tyler raised his head and looked at her, at the moisture squeezing from beneath her lashes. ''Erin? Am I...?''

''No,'' she whispered. ''It doesn't hurt...it's wonderful. So perfect. Don't stop,'' she ended on a plea.

''Never,'' he said, and thrust into her again and again, carrying her with him to mindless ecstasy.

Eventually Tyler relaxed against her, kissing her softly and murmuring into her ear, though she couldn't understand what he was saying. After a minute, he took a deep breath, turned them both to ease the strain on his leg, and nestled her against him.

Reaching down, he grabbed her sleeping bag and spread it over them both.

"Go to sleep," he said, cuddling her into his arms. "It's going to be a long night."

Erin listened to the strong, steady pounding of his heart and felt his arousal beginning once again. She smiled against his chest. "I know," she said.

"ERIN, WAKE UP. I hear something."

She groaned, stretched places that had never been so tender before and murmured, "I hate waking up. Why do you always do this to me?"

"Erin. I hear a horse. You've got to get up. I may need your help."

The urgency in his voice finally communicated itself to her. She sat up, blinking and saw that Tyler was dressed. The moonlight filtering through the branches that hid them illuminated the hard lines of his face. This wasn't the man who had made love to her three times in the past few hours. This man was a stranger.

"Get dressed," Tyler ordered softly, and she obeyed, easing into her clothes as quietly as possible, and slipping into her socks and sneakers. She wasn't even going to think about the way she had broken her own cardinal rule about getting involved with an employer. That was a load of guilt she couldn't shoulder right now.

"What is it?" she asked shakily, reacting to the grimness in his face. She came to stand beside him and peer through the branches into the darkness. She couldn't see a thing.

"I think our rustler is here. I heard hooves on that slide of loose shale." Moving cautiously Tyler stepped forward and peered into the darkness. "Horseback," he muttered. "I would have thought he'd be in his truck."

Erin, trying to adjust to the sudden change from intimacy to the business of catching a rustler, couldn't concentrate on what he was saying. She gave him a blank look, finished tucking her shirt into her jeans and said, "I'm ready."

"I'd rather you stayed here," he admitted in a harsh tone. "But I may need you and I don't think there'll be any real danger."

"I understand," she said, though she really didn't. She was alarmed by his implacable tone.

He held the branches of the willow back for her to pass through, then joined her in the shadows. He carried a big, heavy-duty flashlight that could convert to a lantern, but he didn't turn it on yet. He had rolled the leg of his jeans down over the cast so its white-ness wouldn't gleam in the darkness. He still moved more awkwardly than he would have liked. Erin gave him a concerned look. The set of his shoulders looked as if he was braced for a blow. She wondered if he'd brought a weapon.

Peering into the darkness, it wasn't long before Erin saw what Tyler had seen. The rustler moved from moonlight into shadow, his face hidden by the brim of his hat, his body rangy and loose in the saddle, but leaning forward with purpose. He reached the floor of the valley and started across to the herd. Even in the dim light, Erin could see that he studied them carefully, as if looking for just the right ones.

Tyler put his mouth close to Erin's ear. "He doesn't want nursing heifers. Their calves might come bawling after their mamas. He's probably looking for my prize Brangus bull, the ungrateful bastard. He'll figure out soon enough that the bull's not here, then he'll take some yearlings.''

Erin gave him a puzzled look. "How do you know that?"

Tyler didn't answer, but motioning for her to follow, he made his way across the small valley floor, taking cover when necessary, though he didn't try to mask the sounds they were making. An intruder in their midst had alerted the cattle, who were up and milling around as the rustler tried to cut the best of them from the herd. The noise they made drowned out all other sounds.

Tyler and Erin stepped carefully, with him leaning on her for support occasionally. Erin was amazed that he could move so quietly in his walking cast, but the set of his jaw and the determination in his step told her he wouldn't have been slowed down even if he'd still been on crutches.

They continued to move in cautiously until they were close enough to see the lone rustler. Tyler drew Erin behind a basalt outcropping that gave them a good view of the man. He was tall, whipcord lean and was wearing a dark hat low over his eyes. He seemed to be an expert horseman, turning his mount this way and that as he cut out a big yearling and headed it toward the mouth of the valley. When he passed them, Tyler simply stood, reached out and grabbed the horse's bridle. He flipped on the flashlight at the same moment, and shone it into the man's face.

"Hello, Earl," he said, holding tightly as the man grunted in surprise, the horse shied, then settled and the yearling circled and headed back to the herd.

Erin's mouth dropped open.

"Ty," the man exclaimed. "What...what are you doing here?"

"Looks like I'm catching a rustler." He switched the flashlight into the hand that held the bridle, and shone it into the man's face, then reached up and grabbed him by the arm. "Get down," he said, dragging him to the ground.

Earl half fell from the saddle, stumbling, then righting himself. He looked frightened and rightly so, Erin thought, because Tyler looked more furious than she'd ever seen him. She suspected Earl had never seen him this way before, either.

"Now, this isn't what you think, Ty. I heard you were having some trouble, so I came on out to—"

"Don't bother, Earl. I knew it was you." Tyler's words snapped in the air like dry twigs. "I've known it for a couple of weeks now. You knew I'd broken my leg so I wouldn't be out riding like I usually am, and you knew I'd moved part of my herd up on Diamond Creek because I told you that I was going to the last time we talked."

Earl held his hands out. "Oh, no, Ty, I—"

"Shut up," Tyler said, losing the minimal control he'd held on his temper. "Just shut up."

Alarmed, Erin reached up and touched his arm. She didn't know what she would have said, but he shook her off. She was hurt, though she knew this wasn't the time for her personal feelings.

"Why have you been doing this?" Tyler demanded. He set the light on the ground and adjusted it so it would work as a lantern. Light glowed around them, illuminating Tyler's fury and Earl's fright. Erin got her first good look at Earl's face and understood why Shara had fallen for this tall, good-looking cow-boy when she'd been so young.

When Earl didn't answer him, Tyler said, "Well?"

Earl slumped and, in spite of what he'd done, Erin felt sorry for him. "I need the money, Ty. I haven't made much on the circuit, hardly anything, in fact. I've gotta have some money for Shara and the kids."

"And the only way you could think of to get it is to steal from me?" Tyler demanded. "Me!"

"I...I know we've been friends for a long time," Earl said in a whining tone. "And you've been watching out for Shara and the kids, but I was gonna pay you back as soon as I was able, Ty. Really I was."

Tyler made a sound of deep frustration and anger and Earl rushed on. "I have to have the money, oth-erwise Shara is gonna leave me for sure."

"She should. Why should she stay married to a thief?" Tyler demanded.

Along with the fury in his voice, Erin heard hurt and sick disappointment. This was one of his best friends, a man he had shared many experiences with, one who had saved Tyler's life. She could only imag-ine the disillusionment he must be feeling.

Tyler stabbed a finger at his friend's chest. "I'm going to have you arrested, Earl. Arrested and jailed."

"Aw, Ty, no," the man pleaded. "Think what that would do to Shara and the boys. I'll pay you back."

"I'm going back to the house and calling the sher-iff," Tyler went on in an inexorable tone. "I'll tell him exactly where to find you. I suspect you've been camping on your land, driving the cattle over there, loading them into your truck and hauling them off, right?" When Earl didn't answer, Tyler grabbed his shirt and shook him. "Right?"

"Yeah, Ty, yeah. That's what I did."

Tyler released him with a growl of contempt. "You can explain your whole method to the sheriff when he finds you."

Once again, Erin felt compelled to intervene because Tyler was too furious to be rational.

She reached out to him again and gripped his arm until his glittering eyes turned to her, though they didn't seem to focus.

"Don't do this, Tyler. Give yourself some time to think about this."

"Yeah, Ty," Earl said querulously, recognizing an ally, though he didn't know who she was. "Listen to her."

"There are other ways to solve this," Erin went on. "Shara's going to find a job soon to support herself and the boys. Earl can get one, too, and start paying you...."

"Yeah, yeah, Tyler, listen to her," Earl encouraged again.

"This isn't your business, Erin," Tyler rapped out, then he stepped closer to her and dropped his voice so that only she could hear. "Don't start thinking you can tell me what to do just because I slept with you. It doesn't give you any rights here."

Hurt stabbed through her. Erin leaned in as if she'd been punched in the stomach. How could he say something like that? She opened her mouth to protest, but words wouldn't come out. He only stared at her, his face like carved granite. With a shake of her head, Erin turned and stumbled away toward their camp. When she reached it, she stood for a moment, staring around until she realized she was looking at their sleeping bags, still tossed intimately together. The hurt almost crippled her as tears filled her eyes and began spilling over.

Whirling, she hurried out of the camp, then out of the valley. She left everything behind, including her small overnight bag. It contained a few toiletries that could be easily replaced. She didn't want to carry anything that would slow her down.

Dawn was just beginning to paint the sky and when she looked back, she could see Tyler and Earl standing by the horse, their straight postures and tense movements telling her they were still arguing. She could have driven Tyler's truck, but starting its powerful engine would have alerted him that she was leaving. Not that he would care, but she didn't want him accusing her of taking his truck and leaving him stranded.

She had been every kind of a fool, she berated herself as she rushed over the desert toward home. She knew better than to fall in love with him, but she'd done it anyway. She had certainly known better than to make love with him, but she'd done that, too. She'd ignored her own rules about getting involved with the boss and was suffering the consequences.

Tyler had plainly told her that he was a loner, a man who wanted to be left on his own to live his life, build his ranch as he saw fit. He wanted no interference from her, and he certainly didn't want any love.

Erin reached the house more quickly than she would have expected. She rushed to her room, grabbed her suitcase and began stuffing her things into it. The only thing she could do was leave. She had fulfilled her obligation to Miss Eugenia, stayed almost until Tyler was well—surely that was enough. If not, she would go back to her old method of paying the lady back.

She would call James Westin, Erin thought hysterically as she hastily wrapped two freshly laundered T-shirts around her blow dryer and tossed the lump into her suitcase. He would know about a job for her. This time it would be with someone like the Mornfields: a staid, established couple where her duties would be carefully laid out and there would be none of this fraternizing that had caused her so much trouble.

With tears streaming down her face, she grabbed her suitcase and handbag and staggered toward the door, her car and freedom from Tyler Morris, the man who had made her love him and then broken her heart.

WHERE WAS ERIN? Tyler looked around the camp as the sun came up, touching the Pinalenos with gold and pink light. He had seen her come in this direction, he thought, looking around in some confusion. But the truck was still here, tucked back in the wash where they'd hidden it, so he thought she must be, too.

He moved awkwardly around the campsite until he spied her tracks leading away, toward the house.

What had he said to her? He'd been so furious at Earl that he could barely remember what he'd said to Erin. Thinking about it now, he realized that it was some jackass-brained idiocy about her not having any rights to tell him what to do.

He winced as he moved toward the truck, climbed in and started the engine. It took some maneuvering of his casted foot, but he finally discovered that if he was careful, he could press the gas pedal and still operate the clutch with his left foot to change gears. He slipped the vehicle into four-wheel drive and came up out of the wash. He was leaving their camping gear behind, but it didn't matter. Urgency pushed him to find Erin before what he'd said did too much damage.

What had he been thinking when he said that to her? He'd realized in the night that she was what he wanted and it wasn't because of the sex—though that had been damned good. She was smart and funny, and strong. She wasn't afraid to stand up to him.

He topped a rise and turned toward the house. So why hadn't she stuck around and fought it out with him, since she seemed to be so good at standing up to him?

He knew the answer to that. Because they'd made love and she was in love with him and he'd been too much of a damned fool to tell her so, and to keep his anger at Earl under control.

Tyler turned the truck into the ruts of an old road that ran the length of his property. He'd never had Erin drive it because he was afraid she couldn't handle the truck on such a rough road, but he took it now, guiding the vehicle over the desert until he could see the barn and the house.

As he approached, and circled the hill behind the house, he sat up straight, alarmed that he couldn't see her car. He hadn't been stupid enough to drive her away, had he?

He pulled around the barn in a swirl of dust and

started down the driveway. Halfway, he saw her car, which had nose-dived into the bar ditch that ran the length of the lane. His heart pummeled its way into his throat until he saw that she was unhurt, standing beside it with a distressed and helpless look on her face. When she heard the truck, she looked up. Surprise and hurt flared in her eyes as she turned away from him and started hurrying toward Shara's house.

Cursing himself for a fool, he called out, "Erin, wait."

She didn't even slow down, so he drove up beside her.

"What does a man have to do to get you to listen to him?"

"Send a letter," she snapped.

He leaned out the window and waved his arm at her. "Erin, I'm trying to apologize."

"Hah!" She crossed to the other side of the lane so she wouldn't be so accessible and continued stomping along.

He'd seen angry women before, but no one this furious. It didn't help that he knew he deserved her fury. He tried again. "Erin, slow down."

She spared him a contemptuous glance. "Go suck an egg."

So much for refinement, he thought, suddenly fighting the urge to laugh. She must love him or she wouldn't be so mad at him. Time to play on her pity.

Tyler stopped the truck and climbed out. "Have a heart, Erin," he said plaintively. "I can't walk as fast as you can."

"Good." She glanced back and he didn't see any change in her expression, but she lessened her pace.

"I'm sorry for what I said. I was a jerk."

"Tell me something I don't know," she answered, but her feet slowed to a stop. She looked over her shoulder at him.

"You don't know that I love you."

Stunned, Erin turned to face him. "What?"

"I said I love you." He held out his hands. "And I've never said that to anyone before."

She clamped her hands onto her hips and said, "I've got news for you, cowboy. Love isn't words. It isn't even feelings. It's behavior. Actions."

"I'm learning that." He ran his hand through his hair. "Hell, I always seem to say the wrong thing to you."

"Then...then stop doing it."

He took a deep breath. "I'm sorry I acted like a bastard a while ago. You were right. Shara and the kids will be hurt if I press charges against him, so Earl and I have worked things out. He's going to move his family to Phoenix. He and Shara will get jobs and he'll pay me back. I should have listened to you, but..."

She took a step toward him. Was this Tyler Morris apologizing, telling her that he loved her? She could hardly believe it. "You were hurt by what he'd done—and angry," she said.

"Yeah, but I shouldn't have taken it out on you."

Erin's pace speeded up until she was approaching him at a run. His arms flew out to catch her. His mouth found hers in a desperate kiss. "I love you," he said between small, biting kisses. "I promise I'll never be such a jackass again if you'll stay with me."

Joy rushed through her as she pulled back and looked into his face. "Stay?" she asked on a breathless note. "Stay here?"

"And marry me," he confirmed, kissing her again.

Erin put her hand to her head to stop its spinning. "Marry you?"

He gave her a look that was tinged with worry. "You do love me, don't you?"

"Oh, yes." She kissed him and hugged him tight. "I feel like I've loved you forever."

"Then marry me. Stay here. Help me build this ranch. Make a life with me." His mouth lingered on hers. "And when you're ready, have my children."

"Yes," she said again, leaning into him and giving him another hug. Then she looked up at him and her eyes sparkled with delight. "After all, Sam has the wedding plans all made."

With a laugh, Tyler turned her toward the truck and helped her in. They headed home together.

Catch more great
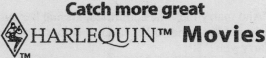
HARLEQUIN™ Movies

featured on the movie channel tmc

Premiering October 10th
Loving Evangeline
Based on the novel by *New York Times* bestselling author Linda Howard

Don't miss next month's movie!
Premiering November 14th
Broken Lullaby
Starring Mel Harris and Rob Stewart.
Based on the novel by bestselling author Laurel Pace

If you are not currently a subscriber to The Movie Channel, simply call your local cable or satellite provider for more details. Call today, and don't miss out on the romance!

 **HARLEQUIN®**
Makes any time special ™

100% pure movies.
100% pure fun.

Harlequin, Joey Device, Makes any time special and Superromance are trademarks of Harlequin Enterprises Limited. The Movie Channel is a trademark of Showtime Networks, Inc., a Viacom Company.

An Alliance Television Production

PHMBPA1096

Can tossing a coin in the Trevi Fountain really make wishes come true? Three average American women are about to find out when they throw...

3 COINS IN A FOUNTAIN

For Gina, Libby and Jessie, the trip to Rome wasn't what they'd expected. They went seeking romance and ended up finding disaster! What harm could throwing a coin bring?

IF WISHES WERE HUSBANDS...
Debbi Rawlins—September

IF WISHES WERE WEDDINGS...
Karen Toller Whittenburg—October

IF WISHES WERE DADDIES...
Jo Leigh—November

3 COINS IN A FOUNTAIN
If wishes could come true...

HARLEQUIN®
Makes any time special ™

Available at your favorite retail outlet.

Look us up on-line at: http://www.romance.net   HAR3C

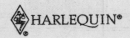

Not The Same Old Story!

 Exciting, glamorous
romance stories that take
readers around the world.

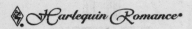 Sparkling, fresh and ten-
der love stories that
bring you pure romance.

 Bold and adventurous—
Temptation is strong women,
bad boys, great sex!

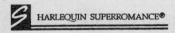 Provocative and realistic
stories that celebrate life
and love.

 Contemporary
fairy tales—where
anything is possible
and where dreams
come true.

 Heart-stopping, suspenseful
adventures that combine the
best of romance and mystery.

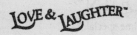 Humorous and romantic stories
that capture the lighter side of
love.

Look us up on-line at: http://www.romance.net   HGENERIC

Don't miss these Harlequin favorites by some of our bestselling authors!

HT#25721	THE ONLY MAN IN WYOMING	$3.50 U.S.	☐
	by Kristine Rolofson	$3.99 CAN.	☐
HP#11869	WICKED CAPRICE	$3.50 U.S.	☐
	by Anne Mather	$3.99 CAN.	☐
HR#03438	ACCIDENTAL WIFE	$3.25 U.S.	☐
	by Day Leclaire	$3.75 CAN.	☐
HS#70737	STRANGERS WHEN WE MEET	$3.99 U.S.	☐
	by Rebecca Winters	$4.50 CAN.	☐
HI#22405	HERO FOR HIRE	$3.75 U.S.	☐
	by Laura Kenner	$4.25 CAN.	☐
HAR#16673	ONE HOT COWBOY	$3.75 U.S.	☐
	by Cathy Gillen Thacker	$4.25 CAN.	☐
HH#28952	JADE	$4.99 U.S.	☐
	by Ruth Langan	$5.50 CAN.	☐
LL#44005	STUCK WITH YOU	$3.50 U.S.	☐
	by Vicki Lewis Thompson	$3.99 CAN.	☐

(limited quantities available on certain titles)

AMOUNT	$ _____
POSTAGE & HANDLING	$ _____
($1.00 for one book, 50¢ for each additional)	
APPLICABLE TAXES*	$ _____
TOTAL PAYABLE	$ _____
(check or money order—please do not send cash)	

To order, complete this form and send it, along with a check or money order for the total above, payable to Harlequin Books, to: **In the U.S.:** 3010 Walden Avenue, P.O. Box 9047, Buffalo, NY 14269-9047; **In Canada:** P.O. Box 613, Fort Erie, Ontario, L2A 5X3.

Name: _____

Address: _____ City: _____

State/Prov.: _____ Zip/Postal Code: _____

Account Number (if applicable): _____

*New York residents remit applicable sales taxes.
Canadian residents remit applicable GST and provincial taxes.

Look us up on-line at: http://www.romance.net

HBLAJ98

HARLEQUIN SUPERROMANCE®

FINDERS, KEEPERS

is a detective agency that specializes in finding lost loves, friends, family, etc...

If Noah had been adventurous enough to discover the world and himself, he could be adventurous enough to visit an agency that specialized in finding lost lovers. But meeting Maggie Tyrell, proprietor, was an adventure in itself. However, Maggie wouldn't be deterred from the task at hand—even if Noah wanted her to call off the search. *Even if it meant her heart would break...*

Found: One Wife

Harlequin Superromance (#809)
October 1998

by Judith Arnold

Available wherever Harlequin books are sold.

HARLEQUIN®

Look us up on-line at: http://www.romance.net

HSRFKOW

HARLEQUIN ULTIMATE GUIDES™

A series of how-to books for today's woman.

Act now to order some of these extremely
helpful guides just for you!

*Whatever the situation, Harlequin Ultimate Guides™
has all the answers!*

#80507	HOW TO TALK TO A	$4.99 U.S. ☐
	NAKED MAN	$5.50 CAN. ☐
#80508	I CAN FIX THAT	$5.99 U.S. ☐
		$6.99 CAN. ☐
#80510	WHAT YOUR TRAVEL AGENT	$5.99 U.S. ☐
	KNOWS THAT YOU DON'T	$6.99 CAN. ☐
#80511	RISING TO THE OCCASION	
	More Than Manners: Real Life	$5.99 U.S. ☐
	Etiquette for Today's Woman	$6.99 CAN. ☐
#80513	WHAT GREAT CHEFS	$5.99 U.S. ☐
	KNOW THAT YOU DON'T	$6.99 CAN. ☐
#80514	WHAT SAVVY INVESTORS	$5.99 U.S. ☐
	KNOW THAT YOU DON'T	$6.99 CAN. ☐
#80509	GET WHAT YOU WANT OUT OF	$5.99 U.S. ☐
	LIFE—AND KEEP IT!	$6.99 CAN. ☐

(quantities may be limited on some titles)

TOTAL AMOUNT $ _____
POSTAGE & HANDLING $ _____
($1.00 for one book, 50¢ for each additional)
APPLICABLE TAXES* $ _____
TOTAL PAYABLE $ _____
(check or money order—please do not send cash)

To order, complete this form and send it, along with a check or money
order for the total above, payable to Harlequin Ultimate Guides, to:
In the U.S.: 3010 Walden Avenue, P.O. Box 9047, Buffalo, NY
14269-9047; **In Canada:** P.O. Box 613, Fort Erie, Ontario, L2A 5X3.

Name: _____

Address: _____ City: _____

State/Prov.: _____ Zip/Postal Code: _____

*New York residents remit applicable sales taxes.
Canadian residents remit applicable GST and provincial taxes.

❖ HARLEQUIN®

Look us up on-line at: http://www.romance.net

HNFBL4

Humorous love stories by favorite authors and brand-new stars!

These books are delightful romantic comedies featuring the lighter side of love. Whenever you want to escape and enjoy a few chuckles and a wonderful love story, choose Love & Laughter.

Love & Laughter—always romantic...always entertaining.

Available at your favorite retail outlet.

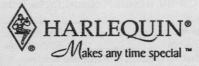

HARLEQUIN®
Makes any time special ™

Look us up on-line at: http://www.romance.net   HLLGEN